An Editing Workbook for Chinese Technical Writers

科技英文編修訓練手冊

By Ted Knoy
柯　泰　德

清蔚科技股份有限公司　出版事業部

This book is dedicated to my wife, Hwang Li-Wen.

序言

　　「科技英文寫作」是一項非常重要的技巧。台灣目前正積極加入各種世界組織，尋求國際發展。科技的強弱是關鍵性的一環。但是有了科技的實質成就，如何把研究成果用英文精確的展現出來，是每一個科技學者應具有的能力。

　　本書是要針對台灣科技研究人員在英文寫作發表這方面的訓練，書中的各單元練習逐步、漸次地訓練作者科技英文寫作編修能力及糾正中國人在科技英文寫作上常犯的錯誤，包括文法、格式、及一些口語習慣，使其所發表的文章更為精確。此外，本書亦為國立清華大學資訊工程系非同步遠距教學的教材範本。

　　台灣的科技文獻每每因為英文問題在國際期刊發表的過程中，反反覆覆的修改而浪費了許多寶貴的時間資源，本書以實用性練習對症下藥，期望科技英文寫作者熟能生巧，實在是一個很有用的教材。

國立清華大學校長

劉 炯 朗

1999 年 12 月 24 日

彭旭明—國立台灣大學副校長

本書為科技英文寫作系列之四；以練習題為主，由反覆練習中提升寫作及編輯能力。適合理、工、醫、農的學生及研究人員使用，特為推薦。

許千樹—國立交通大學研究發展處研發長

處於今日高科技的時代，國人用到科技英文寫作之機會甚多，如何能以精練的手法寫出一篇好的科技論文，極為重要。本書針對國人寫作之缺點提供了各種清楚的編修範例，實用性高，極具參考價值。

陳文村—國立清華大學電機資訊學院院長

處在我國日益國際化、資訊化的社會裡，英文書寫是必備的基本能力，本書提供很多極具參考價值的範例。柯泰德先生在清大任教科技英文寫作多年，深受學生喜愛，本人樂於推薦此書。

韓復華—國立交通大學管理學院院長

二十一世紀將進入數位化經濟體網路全面普及化的電子時代，我們將面臨更大的國際全球化的競爭壓力，同時也將更需要有良好的科技英文寫作能力。本書以實例修正對比的方式作成訓練手冊，一方面列出國人寫作易犯的錯失，避免讀者重蹈覆轍，另一方面明確提供對應的正確用詞與句型；實用而有價值，亦有助於提昇讀者二十一世紀全球化的知識競爭力。

沈文仁—國立交通大學電機資訊學院院長

本書以實用的例子編輯成許多練習題，來引入文件編修的技巧，使讀者能避免常犯的寫作格式錯誤，進而能以更明確的方式來表達意念，是科技英文寫作中十分值得參考的一本好書。

許友耕—工研院行政服務中心主任

對多數國人來說，英文要寫的簡潔、準確是非常不容易的事，坊間的書籍多為原則說明，並不實用；本書作者萃取其多年英文教學與修改的經驗，針對國人習見的問題，從實例下手，讓您在短時間內掌握英文編修的重點，堪稱是實用且有效。

王偉中—財團法人自強工業科學基金會執行長

近年來，我國科技研發人員將研發成果投稿至國外期刊鉅增，不少研究報告或文件，甚至博士論文亦在國際化的趨勢下，多必需以英文撰寫，而如何以英文適切表達自己的意念常是研發人員的頭痛問題。本書藉由精編的演習題，提供了讀者如何強化精簡文句的功力，如何善用主動語法，如何善用動詞等建議，讓讀者可在最短的時間內學得正確的寫作格式，頗具實用價值，特為推薦。

蘇宗粲—工研院化學工業研究所副所長

科技英文寫作是科技人員在追求國際化目標必需的一個過程。本書提供許多寫作型式、內容結構之範例，介紹文件編輯技巧，頗為實用，對提昇科技人員寫作技巧甚具參考價值。

周大新—中研院化學所所長

本國人以非母語的英文寫作時，難免會遇到許多語法上的問題。這種困境最好的改進方法，只有多聽、多看、多寫、和多思考。柯泰德先生的著作提供許多的實例，讓我們能反覆比較各種句型的差異和優劣，這種練習對於英文寫作的技巧甚為俾益。

黃能富—國立清華大學資訊工程研究所所長

本書提供有關科技英文寫作之指引與實例，對於科技論文之撰寫與提昇科技表達能力都有相當助益，是極具參考價值之工具書。

羅濟群—國立交通大學資訊管理研究所所長

科技文稿之表，應避冗贅，如何將一份簡潔精確之用語表達予報告文件，無關乎學力，其道雖小，若因此而造成文稿被拒或延遲實為憾事。本書針對時下一般科技人常見的寫作錯誤，集結範例，詳細詮釋，使自修者有無師自通之樂，極力推薦。

張仲儒—國立交通大學電信工程學系主任

論文及技術文件的撰寫，在學術研究及產品開發均扮演重要的角色。本書除敘述如何有效地編修稿件外，並同時說明若干寫作的觀念與技巧，是學術界及產業界同仁值得參考的好書。

宋光夫—奇美食品股份有限公司董事長

置身於科技與資訊的新紀元，溝通的技巧首重簡潔與效率。特別是面對英文為主的國際技藝交流。合宜的文詞表達與深厚的研發技術，可達相得益彰之效果。柯泰德先生的專業與用心藉著陸續引介的科技英文寫作系列，為台灣科技界提供了適時的參考，特為推薦。

Table of Contents

UNIT Five   Avoid Overusing Sentences that Begin with It and There 96

避免過度使用 It 及 There 開頭句

使用 It 及 There 開頭的句子容易使文章語多累贅及曖昧不清。除非 It 指的是先前句子所提特定的名詞，否則應完全地避免 It is 的句型。數個由 It is 開頭的句型應去除掉，因爲他們對句意並沒幫助。如果不能完全省略去除掉這種句型，則應更爲精簡地描述全句。

UNIT Six   Delete Redundant and Needless Phrases 118

除去重複及不必要的措詞

這些擾人重複不必要的文詞其實可以完全去除，或是用更簡明的方式 表達。

本書同時是國立清華大學資訊工程學系非同步遠距教學科技英文寫作課程指導手册

Foreword

Technical writing is an essential tool for garnering international recognition of accomplishments made by Taiwan's technical and scientific community. To meet this need, "The Chinese Technical Writers Series" seeks to provide a sound technical writing curriculum and, on a more practical level, to provide valuable reference guides for Chinese technical and managerial professionals. The Series concentrates on aiding Chinese technical writers in the following areas:

Writing style

The books in the Series seek to transform archaic ways of writing (often resulting from literally copying phrases from other texts) into a more active and direct writing style that makes the author's main ideas easier to identify.

Structure and content

Another issue facing technical writers is how to organize the structure and contents of manuscripts and other common forms of writing in the workplace. The exercises in this workbook should help writers to avoid and correct stylistic errors commonly found in technical documents.

Quality

Technical writers must inevitably prepare their manuscripts to meet the expectations of editors, referees and reviewers, as well as to satisfy journal requirements. The books in this Series are prepared with these specific needs in mind.

An Editing Workbook for Chinese Technical Writers is the fourth book in the Chinese Technical Writers Series.

『An Editing Workbook for Chinese Technical Writers』爲「科技英文寫作系列（The Chinese Technical Writers Series）」之第四本書，本手冊中練習題部份主要是幫助科技英文作者避免及糾正常犯寫作格式上錯誤，由反覆練習中，進而熟能生巧提升寫作及編修能力。

「科技英文寫作系列」針對以下內容逐步協助中國人解決在科技英文寫作上所遭遇之各項問題：

A．寫作型式：把往昔通常習於抄襲的寫作方法轉換成更主動積極的寫作方式，俾使讀者所欲表達的主題意念更加清楚。

B．方法型式：指出國內寫作者從事英文寫作或英文翻譯時常遇到的文法問題。

C．內容結構：將科技寫作的內容以下面的方式結構化：工程目標、工程動機、個人動機。並了解不同的目的和動機可以影響論文的結構，由此，獲得最適當的論文內容。

D．內容品質：以編輯、審查委員的要求來寫作此一系列之書籍，以滿足期刊的英文要求。

本手冊乃是科技英文寫作系列中第四本著作，其他尚有
　　1.精通科技論文（報告）寫作之捷徑
　　2.作好英語會議簡報
　　3.英文信函參考手冊

Introduction

Concise writing in technical documents does not occur automatically. Several rough drafts may be required before the author is finally ready to send the document off for publication. Somewhere along the process, the document may end up on an editor's desk to refine the author's meaning for conciseness.

This editing workbook introduces copyediting skills in a practical format. Upon completing the exercises in the book, the writer should have a better idea of how to refine his or her intended meaning by omitting stylstic errors commonly found in a technical document.

The exercises in this workbook are part of the technical writing course offered at the Department of Computer Science, National Tsing Hua University. In addition to the Guide toTechnical Writing Curriculum provided at the end of this book, further details regarding the course can be found via the World Wide Web at http://mx.nthu.edu.tw/~tedknoy .

要把科技英文寫得精確並不是件容易的事情。通常在文稿投寄發表前,作者都要不斷反覆修飾原稿避免辭不達意的窘境,由於這過程是如此的繁複,最後甚至需請專業人士代為編修始能清楚闡述作者原意。

有鑑於此,本手冊希望以最實用的方式來介紹文件編修的技巧,並透過編修訓練避免英文寫作上常犯的錯誤。本手冊分為六大單元,依次針對「精確寫作」(Write for Conciseness)、「常用主動語氣」(Use Active Voice Frequently)、「動詞替代名詞」(Use Verbs Instead of Nouns)、「強有力的動詞」(Create Strong Verbs)、「避免過度使用It 及There開頭句」(Avoid Overusing Sentences that Begin with *It* and *There*)、「除去重複及不必要的措詞」(Delete Redundant and Needless Phrases)等科技英文寫作要點提供二十七個實用的練習章節。

每個練習章節 (Exercise) 皆提供 10-15 題不等的編修練習題,提供您直接修改文法、句型、單字用語等常犯錯誤，再參考每個練習章節後所附的解答 (Answer)。本手冊的解答皆由作者親自編修，提供您教師隨堂講解的功能；每個練習題皆附有建議寫作方式及作者寫作提示 (Editor's Note)，讓您可以快速學習各項科技英文寫作技巧。

　　本手冊提供您一個簡易的方式學習科技英文寫作，當您做完全部的練習章節後，將可以有效的避免各種常犯的寫作格式錯誤，進而提升科技英文寫作的表達能力。本手冊同時為國立清華大學資訊工程學系科技英文寫作課程指導範本，您可以參考網頁上的詳細資料，網址為：http://mx.nthu.edu.tw/~tedknoy。

Copy editing marks used in this Workbook

修改前句子	修改後句子	修改符號的代表意義
Gett ridd of wordiness.	Get rid of wordiness.	**_Delete_**　刪除
Make ideas ideas clear.	Make ideas clear.	
new information Add to a sentence.	Add new information to a sentence.	**_Insert_**　插入文字
new information Add to a sentence.	Add new information to a sentence.	
Omitredundancy.	Omit redundancy.	**_Insert space_**　插入空格
Omitredundancy.	Omit redundancy.	
Telecommunications	telecommunications	**_Lower case_**　大寫改成小寫
TELECOMMUNICATIONS	telecommunications	
microsoft	Microsoft	**_Capitals_**　小寫改成大寫
ibm	IBM	
Craete srtong verbs.	Create strong verbs.	**_Transpose_**　前後對調
strong Create verbs.	Create strong verbs.	
in a sentence. Strong verbs should be created	Strong verbs should be created in a sentence.	**_Brackets_**　括號
Create strong verbs ⊙	Create strong verbs.	**_Period_**　句點

Unit One

Write for Conciseness

精確寫作

Conciseness in technical writing is essential for busy professionals who do not have the time to read wordy documents. Technical documents are often rejected or their publication is delayed simply because the writer could not express his or her intended meaning in as few words as possible. Writing a long document is often easier than writing a short one because writing concisely takes longer than simply writing. When editing a document for conciseness, the writer faces the challenge of expressing the technical contents as succinctly as possible.

The exercises in this unit quiz the writer on his or her ability to simplify sentences in a technical document.

忙碌的專家們是沒有時間去逐字的閱讀冗長的報告文件，因此很多科技作者的文稿被拒絕或延遲發表，就是因為他們無法精短的表達文章意念。本單元即要強化您精簡文句的功力。

Exercise 1

Correct the following sentences using the copyediting marks on page **XIV** .

1.　All inputs are combined by engineers to create a

　　product.

2.　Three phases of analysis are included in their approach.

3.　A statistical comparison is made of the proposed procedures with

　　Taguchi's two-step procedure.

4.　A more efficient combination among the factor levels is

　　achieved when the control factor is continuous.

5.　Factors causing saturation include temperature, volume

　　and weight.

6.　The Taguchi approach entails minimizing the average

　　quadratic loss.

7. There has been a considerable amount of studies on

    robust design.

8. There is a significant difference in control levels for the

    parameter settings.

9. The committee made a decision on the question as to using

    an individual mouse or a trackball would be more

    productive.

10. As a general rule, mice and trackballs serve the function of

    being both used for the same reason.

Answers

Exercise 1

1. ~~All inputs are combined by~~ engineers to create a product.

Engineers combine all inputs to create a product.

EDITOR'S NOTE 1.1 Switching from passive voice to active voice makes the sentence more direct, concise and persuasive.

2. ~~Three phases of analysis are included in their approach.~~

Their approach includes three phases of analysis.

EDITOR'S NOTE 1.2 Like in the previous sentence, using passive voice makes the sentence wordy or indecisive. However, active voice makes the sentence more direct and clear.

3. ~~A statistical comparison is made of~~ the proposed procedures ~~with~~ Taguchi's two-step procedure.

The proposed procedures and Taguchi's two-step procedure are statistically compared.

EDITOR'S NOTE 1.3 Using a verb instead of a noun simplifies this sentence. Avoid sentences that contain phrases like ***is made, is done, is performed, is conducted, is undertaken*** and ***is achieved*** . Such phrases often make the sentence unnecessarily long. Consider the following examples:

Original
Simulation of the program is done.
Revised
The program is simulated.

Original
Implementation of the program is performed.
Revised
The program is implemented.

Original
Optimization of the output is achieved.
Revised
The output is optimized.

4. A more efficient combination among the factor levels is achieved when the control factor is continuous.

The factor levels are more efficiently combined when the control factor is continuous.

5. Factors causing saturation include temperature, volume and weight.

Temperature, volume and weight cause saturation.

EDITOR'S NOTE 1.4   A writer should use strong verbs that imply a precise action. In this case, *cause* implies a more precise action than *include* . Avoid overusing verbs like *make, come, take, is, are, was, were* which often have a general meaning rather than a precise one. Consider the following examples:
Original (Unclear action)
The purpose of this study is to understand the underlying factors.
Revised (Clear action)
This study attempts (aims) to understand the underlying factors.

> *Original (Unclear action)*
> *The committee made a decision on what to do next.*
> *Revised (Clear action)*
> *The committee decided what to do next.*

6.   The Taguchi approach ~~entails~~ minimiz~~ing~~ the average

quadratic loss.

The Taguchi approach minimizes the average quadratic loss.

7.   ~~There~~ has ~~been a~~ considerable ~~amount of studies on~~ *received* *attention*

robust design.

Robust design has received considerable attention.

> ***EDITOR'S NOTE 1.5*** Writers should try to avoid sentences that start with ***There*** and ***It*** to save space
> and to achieve a greater emphasis. Consider the following examples:
> *Original*
> *There are many programs available in Taiwan.*
> *Revised*
> *Many programs are available in Taiwan.*
>
> *Original*
> *It is possible to create many designs with the software.*
> *Revised*
> *Many designs can be created with the software.*

8.   ~~There is a~~ significant difference in control levels for the

parameter settings.

The parameter settings significantly differ in control levels.

EDITOR'S NOTE 1.6 In the revised sentence, the writer not only avoids the ***There is*** sentence opener but also turns a general verb (*is*) into a precise one (***significantly differ***).

9.   The committee ~~made a decision on the question as to~~ using   *ded   whether*

an ~~individual~~ mouse or a trackball would be more

productive.

The committee decided whether using a mouse or a trackball in the workplace would be more productive.

EDITOR'S NOTE 1.7 The writer should try to avoid needless and redundant words and phrases that only make the sentence lengthy. In addition to using a strong verb that expresses a more precise action (***decided*** instead of ***made a decision***), the revised sentence uses a simpler word instead of a wordy phrase (***whether*** instead of ***the question as to***). Unit Six provides more examples of needless and redundant words and phrases.

10.   As a ~~general~~ rule, mice and trackballs ~~serve the function of~~   *are*

~~being~~ both used for the same reason.

As a rule, mice and trackballs are both used for the same

reason.

EDITOR'S NOTE 1.8 Another form of redundancy is putting two words together that have the same meaning. Since ***rule*** implies something that is ***general*** , the writer can easily cut this phrase in half by simply saying ***rule*** instead of ***general rule*** . More examples are provided in Unit Six.

Exercise 2

Correct the following sentences using the proofreading marks on page **XIV** *.*

1. This concept was further extended in their work to include the conventional approach.

2. A simple modification of these notions was made by Smith et al. for determination of the constructs.

3. For determination of the optimum conditions for the nominal-the-best robust design problems, this work is conducted to develop a simple procedure to do so.

4. A continuous change of flexible manufacturing systems in a dynamic environment occurs.

5. Those factors have a significant effect on the signal-to-noise (SN) ratio.

6.   Leon, Shoemaker and Kacker (1987) provided a justification for the use of the SN ratio and an explanation of why Taguchi's two-step procedure would minimize average loss.

7.   It seems that the optimal factor/level combination is dominated by the maximum quality loss.

8.   There is a slight difference in terms of speed between the two methods.

9.   There can be little doubt that AB is a more stable operating system than CD in order that the user is able to make future predictions of market trends.

10.   There is a need for clarification of organizational goals at such time as the company is capable of entering the global market in the near future.

Answers

Exercise 2

1. 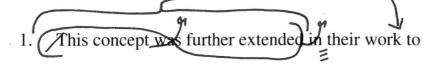 This concept was further extended in their work to

   include the conventional approach.

   Their work further extended this concept to include the
   conventional approach.

   EDITOR'S NOTE 1.9　Putting the sentence in active voice not only saves space and makes the sentence more direct, but also places the most important noun at the front of the sentence.

2. A simple modification of these notions was made by

   Smith et al. for determination of the constructs.

   Smith et al. simply modified these notions to determine
   the constructs.

   EDITOR'S NOTE 1.10　Again, turning nouns into verbs is an easy way of simplifying a sentence.

3. For determination of the optimum conditions for the

   nominal-the-best robust design problems, this work is

   conducted to develop a simple procedure to do so.

   This work develops a simple procedure to determine
   the optimum conditions for the nominal-the-best robust
   design problems.

EDITOR'S NOTE 1.11   Like the original sentence, many writers add unnecessary prefaces in front of the subject. Doing so tends to push the subject away from the front of the sentence and makes it more difficult for the reader to identify. However, in the revised sentence, the subject is placed in front of the sentence by making an unnecessary noun (**determination**) into a verb.

4.   A continuous change of flexible manufacturing systems

in a dynamic environment occurs.

Flexible manufacturing systems continuously change in
a dynamic environment.

EDITOR'S NOTE 1.12   Instead of hiding a verb inside a noun, the revised sentence is simplified and **continuously change** expresses a more direct action than **occurs** .

5.   Those factors have a significant effect on the signal-

to-noise (SN) ratio.

Those factors significantly affect the signal-to-noise
(SN) ratio.

EDITOR'S NOTE 1.13   Omitting **have** makes the action in the sentence clearer.

6.   Leon, Shoemaker and Kacker (1987) provided a justification for the

use of the SN ratio and an explanation of why Taguchi's two-step

procedure would minimize average loss.

Leon, Shoemaker and Kacker (1987) justified using the SN
ratio and explained why Taguchi's two-step procedure
would minimize average loss.

EDITOR'S NOTE 1.14 Turning nouns into verbs makes the sentence less wordy and more direct.

7. It seems that the optimal factor/level combination is dominated by the maximum quality loss.

The maximum quality loss seems to dominate the optimal factor/level combination.

EDITOR'S NOTE 1.15 Avoiding the sentence opener of *It* and changing from passive to active voice greatly simplify this sentence.

8. There is a slight difference in terms of speed between the two methods.

The two methods slightly differ in speed.

EDITOR'S NOTE 1.16 Avoiding *There is* sentence openers not only makes the sentence more direct by putting the subject towards the front of the sentence, but also makes the sentence less wordy. The sentence can be further simplified by watching out for wordy phrases (*in* instead of *in terms of*).

9. There can be little doubt that AB is a more stable operating system than CD in order that the user is able to make future predictions of market trends.

AB is undoubtedly a more stable operating system than CD so the user can predict market trends.

EDITOR'S NOTE 1.17   As the above revision demonstrates, omitting wordy phrases and expressing the same meaning more concisely can greatly simplify a sentence. As mentioned earlier, putting two words together that have the same meaning is another form of redundancy. Redundancy in this sentence is omitted by simply saying *predictions* instead of *future predictions* . Furthermore, turning the noun *predictions* into *predict* further simplifies the sentence.

10.   ~~There is a need for~~ clarification ~~of~~ organizational goals ~~at such time as~~
       must be   *ed*   *when*

       the company ~~is capable of~~ entering the global market ~~in the near~~
       can   *soon*

       ~~future~~

Organizational goals must be clarified when the company
can enter the global market soon.

別忘了休息一下喔！

Exercise 3

Correct the following sentences using the proofreading marks on page .

1. A good layout should not be determined by a single

    period.

2. Heuristics were included in this system to solve the

    dynamic layout problem.

3. Reduction of the number of states is attempted by

    a bounding procedure, but is not successful.

4. Consideration must be made of the two variables.

5. In terms of cost savings, there is no significant difference

    between the control group and the experimental group.

6. Robust design was chosen to be the focus of this study owing to its

    importance during the past twenty years.

Exercise 3

7.   There are many factors that affect product strategy.

8.   It is possible for the system to gather all unknown variables.

9.   The basic essentials of a successful trip are careful advance planning and

     future prediction of any unforeseeable circumstances.

10. The first priority in making a definite decision is that the group can

     reach a consensus of opinion.

11. It is necessary to recognize the increasingly prominent role of the

     Internet in our lives.

12. It is possible to identify parts with similar processing requirements.

Answers

Exercise 3

1. 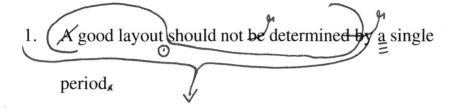 A good layout should not be determined by a single

    period.

    A single period should not determine a good layout.

2. 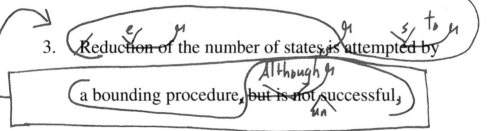 Heuristics were included in this system to solve the

    dynamic layout problem.

    This system included heuristics to solve the dynamic layout

    problem.

3. Reduction of the number of states is attempted by

    a bounding procedure, but is not successful.

    Although unsuccessful, a bounding procedure attempts
    to reduce the number of states.

4. Consideration must be made of the two variables.

    The two variables must be considered.

Exercise 3

5. In terms of cost savings, there is no significant difference between the control group and the experimental group.

The control group and the experimental group do not significantly differ in cost savings.

6. Robust design was chosen to be the focus of this study owing to its importance during the past twenty years. two decades

This study focused on robust design owing to its importance during the past two decades.

7. There are many factors that affect product strategy.

Many factors affect product strategy.

8. It is possible for the system to gather all unknown variables. can

The system can gather all unknown variables.

9. The basic essentials of a successful trip are careful advance planning and future prediction of any unforeseeable circumstances.

The essentials of a successful trip are careful planning and prediction of any unforeseeable circumstances.

10. The first priority in making a ~~definite~~ decision is ~~that~~ the group ~~can~~

    reach a consensus of opinion.

    The priority in making a decision is for the group to reach
    a consensus.

11. ~~It is necessary to~~ recognize the increasingly prominent role of the

    Internet in our lives.

    The increasingly prominent role of the Internet in our lives
    must be recognized.

12. ~~It is essential to~~ identify parts with similar processing requirements.

    Parts with similar processing requirements must be
    identified.

Use Active Voice Frequently

常用主動語氣

As mentioned in the last unit, most technical writers face the challenge of expressing their technical contents succinctly in as few words as possible. A simple way to delete the length of a sentence and make it direct at the same time is to frequently use the active voice. Switching from passive voice to active voice often makes a sentence more direct, concise and persuasive. Whereas sentences using passive voice tend to be wordy or indecisive, sentences utilizing active voice make the technical document more immediate and concise.

就像先前所說，如何用最少的字來表達一個完整的意念通常是科技寫作者一個大挑戰，然而這裡有一個祕訣，那就是使用主動語法。請記住主動語氣使句子更直接，明確及更有說服力。

Consider the following examples:

Original
The optimization of multiple response problems in the Taguchi method is achieved by the proposed procedure.
Revised
The proposed procedure optimizes multiple response problems in the Taguchi method.

Original
Multiple response problems in the Taguchi method are optimized by the proposed procedure.
Revised
The proposed procedure optimizes multiple response problems in the Taguchi method.

Original
The multiple cases are different for each response.
Revised
Each response differs for the multiple cases.

The above revisions demonstrate that in addition to making the sentences shorter, the verb expresses a clearer action than in the original ones. Therefore, using active voice often makes the document easier to read.

以上修正部份除了使原句簡短外，動詞更為清楚。所以使用主動語氣會使整篇文章更明朗。

However, passive voice is preferred when the doer of the action is unknown or unimportant (or less important than the action itself). Consider the following example:

然而，有些情況卻要使用被動語氣，通常是行為者不明或是不重要時。請細想比較以下例句：

A trackball is used to move the position of the cursor around the screen.

In the above sentence, the person who is using the trackball is unknown or unimportant, and definitely less important than the action of moving the trackball. Therefore, in this instance, passive voice is preferred.

在此句中，使用電腦軌跡球的人不知是誰也不重要，重點是球移動的這個事件，所以您知道在這情況下要使用被動語法。

Space is needed to move a trackball.

Similar to the above example, the person who needs space is unknown or important, and definitely less important than the action of needing space to move the trackball.

類似以上的例句，需要這個空間的人不知道是誰也並不重要，重點應放在移動球所需空間的這個事件上，故要使用被動語法。

Exercise 4

Put the following sentences in active voice by using the copyediting marks on page **XIV** .

1. Modification of the heuristics was made by Lacksonen

    and Enscore (1993) to solve the dynamic layout

    problem.

2. Minimization of total operating costs is achieved by a

    planning horizon.

3. A description of the layout cost evaluation method is made

    by introducing the following notations in this section.

4. Precise measurement of neural networks by practitioners

    is a heavy emphasis of computer vision systems.

5. Numerical analysis is performed in this study on the effects

    of the inflation rate and the deterioration rate on stock

    inventory.

6.   The manager can be assisted by the proposed model so that

     the order size can be precisely determined.

7.   The temperature is increased by uncontrollable factors,

     as indicated in the experimental results.

8.   The proposed model can be extended in a future study so that

     more realistic assumptions can be incorporated.

9.   A more detailed description of the three design types is provided in Kackar

     and Phadke (1991).

10. The GRG algorithm may be difficult for users with limited statistical training to

     implement.

11. The server is notified by the website manager that retrieval of the data

     must be performed by the account holder.

Exercise 4

12. Verification of the data accuracy is required by the site manager so that

    quality control within a factory is ensured.

13. Consumer preferences are markedly affected by advertising.

14. Various options are generally made in user choice.

15. Provision of textbook materials should be offered by the instructor.

起來走走動動吧！

Answers

Exercise 4

1. Modification of the heuristics was made by Lacksonen and Enscore (1993) to solve the dynamic layout problem.

Lacksonen and Enscore (1993) modified the heuristics to solve the dynamic layout problem.

> **EDITOR'S NOTE 2.1** In addition to switching to active voice so that the intended meaning is more direct, this sentence also turns a noun into a verb to save further space. Unit 3 provides more practice on turning nouns into verbs to simplify your meaning.

2. Minimization of total operating costs is achieved by a planning horizon.

A planning horizon minimizes total operating costs.

> **EDITOR'S NOTE 2.2** As shown in the original sentence, some writers tend to overuse unnecessary phrases like is **made, is done, is performed, is conducted, is undertaken** and "is achieved" . This often makes the sentence unnecessarily long Omitting such phrases, turning the subject into a verb and switching from passive voice makes this sentence much easier to understand.

3. A description of the layout cost evaluation method is made by introducing the following notations in this section.

This section introduces the following notations to describe the layout cost evaluation method.

4. Precise measurement of neural networks by practitioners is a heavy emphasis of computer vision systems.

Computer vision systems heavily emphasize that practitioners precisely measure computer vision systems.

EDITOR'S NOTE 2.3   Switching from passive voice to active voice and turning two nouns into verbs greatly simplify this sentence.

5. Numerical analysis is performed in this study on the effects of the inflation rate and the deterioration rate on stock inventory.

This study numerically analyzes how inflation and deterioration rates affect stock inventory.

6. The manager can be assisted by the proposed model so that the order size can be precisely determined.

The proposed model can assist the manager in precisely determining the order size.

EDITOR'S NOTE 2.4   To increase word variety in a sentence, the writer can use **assist, facilitate, guide** or **direct** instead of always saying **help** when the Chinese meaning is 幫忙 / 幫助 .

7. The temperature is increased by uncontrollable factors, as indicated in the experimental results.

Experimental results indicate that uncontrollable factors increase the temperature.

8. The proposed model can be extended in a future study so that more realistic assumptions can be incorporated.

A future study can extend the proposed model to incorporate more realistic assumptions.

9. A more detailed description of the three design types is provided in Kackar and Phadke (1991)

Kackar and Phadke (1991) describe the three design types in more detail.

10. The GRG algorithm may be difficult for users with limited statistical training to implement.

Users with limited statistical training may have difficulty in implementing the GRG algorithm.

11. The server is notified by the website manager that retrieval of the data must be performed by the account holder.

The website manager notifies the server that the account
holder must retrieve the data.

12. Verification of the data accuracy is required by the site manager so that

quality control within a factory is ensured.

The site manager must verify the data accuracy to ensure
quality control within a factory.

> **EDITOR'S NOTE 2.5**   Depending on the sentence's context, *verify*, *confirm* and *demonstrate*
> can be used as alternatives to *check* or *prove* when the Chinese meaning is 檢查 / 證明 .
>
> Similarly, depending on the sentence's context, *ensure* and *assure* can be used as alternatives to
> *make sure* when the Chinese meaning is 確定 .

13. Consumer preferences are markedly affected by advertising.

Advertising markedly affects consumer preferences.

> **EDITOR'S NOTE 2.6**   To increase word variety in a sentence, *markedly, significantly, heavily*
> and *substantially* can be used as alternatives to *much, strongly* and *greatly* when the Chinese
> meaning is 很多 / 非常 .

14. Various options are generally made in user choice.

Users generally choose various options.

15. Provision of textbook materials should be offered by the instructor.

The instructor should provide textbook materials.

Exercise 5

Put the following sentences in active voice by using the copyediting marks on page *.*

1. Product and operational procedures are significantly influenced by design parameters and noise factors.

2. More than one feature in most manufactured products is normally made in customer consideration.

3. Determination of the parameter settings should be made by the manufacturer.

4. SN ratios are analyzed in the following section so that the optimal settings of the design parameters can be determined.

5. A thorough review of the multi-response problems in the Taguchi method is made in Section 2.

Exercise 5

6.   Accurate measurement of a multi-response performance is required by

the designer.

7.   A series of steps is included in the proposed optimization procedure for when

the Taguchi method is applied by an engineer.

8.   Selections among some courses of action must be made by the user in

the presence of multiple attributes.

9.   Subjective assessment of the importance of each response by the user

is allowed by the proposed method.

10.   Assessment of a desirability value is impossible by a user under some

circumstances.

11.   Specification of suitable operations is required by a user so that the

responses can be simultaneously optimized.

12. An adjustment in the temperature can be made by the engineer.

13. Relevant statistics are examined in the following section so that the

     underlying factors can be assessed.

14. A detailed description of the economic situation is made in Section 2.

15. Objective assessment of the workplace is required by the supervisor.

站起來活動吧！
免得骨頭僵硬喔～

Answers

Exercise 5

1. Product and operational procedures are significantly influenced by design parameters and noise factors.

Design parameters and noise factors significantly influence product and operational procedures.

EDITOR'S NOTE 2.7   Depending on the sentence's context, *influence* and *impact* can be used as alternatives to *affect* when the Chinese meaning is 影響 .

2. More than one feature in most manufactured products is normally made in customer consideration.

A customer normally considers more than one feature in most manufactured products.

EDITOR'S NOTE 2.8   To increase word variety in a sentence, *normally, typically* and *generally* can be used as alternatives to *usually* when the Chinese meaning is 通常／經常 .

3. Determination of the parameter settings should be made by the manufacturer.

The manufacturer should determine the parameter settings.

4. SN ratios are analyzed in the following section so that the optimal settings of the design parameters can be determined.

The following section analyzes SN ratios to determine the optimal settings of the design parameters.

5. A thorough review of the multi-response problems in the Taguchi method is made in Section 2.

Section 2 thoroughly reviews the multi-response problems in the Taguchi method.

6. Accurate measurement of a multi-response performance is required by the designer.

The designer must accurately measure a multi-response performance.

7. A series of steps is included in the proposed optimization procedure for when the Taguchi method is applied by an engineer.

The proposed optimization procedure includes a series of steps for when an engineer applies the Taguchi method.

EDITOR'S NOTE 2.9   Depending on the sentence's context, *apply/applied, employ/employed,* and *utilize/utilized* can be used as alternatives to *use/used* when the Chinese meaning is 使用 / 被使用 .

32

Exercise 5

8. Selections among some courses of action must be made by the user in
   the presence of multiple attributes.

   The user must select a course of action in the presence of
   multiple attributes.

9. Subjective assessment of the importance of each response by the user
   is allowed by the proposed method.

   The proposed method allows the user to subjectively assess the
   importance of each response.

10. Assessment of a desirability value is impossible by a user under some
    circumstances.

    A user can not assess a desirability value under some
    circumstances.

11. Specification of suitable operations is required by a user so that the
    responses can be simultaneously optimized.

    A user must specify suitable operations to simultaneously
    optimize the responses.

12. An adjustment in the temperature can be made by the engineer.

    The engineer can adjust the temperature.

13. Relevant statistics are examined in the following section so that the underlying factors can be assessed.

The following section examines relevant statistics to assess the underlying factors.

> **EDITOR'S NOTE 2.10**   Depending on the sentence's context, **examines, investigates, explores** and **elucidates** can be used as alternatives to **studies** when the Chinese meaning is 研讀 .

14. A detailed description of the economic situation is made in Section 2.

Section 2 describes the economic situation in detail.

15. Objective assessment of the workplace is required by the supervisor.

The supervisor must objectively assess the workplace.

Exercise 6

Put the following sentences in active voice by using the proofreading marks on page .

1. Operational procedures are manipulated so that

    the parameters can be determined.

2. The Taguchi method is thoroughly assessed so that the

    effect of various factors on performance variation can

    be understood.

3. The function is minimized so that suitable operating

    conditions are satisfied.

4. The single-response problem is focused on so that a

    modification of the operating system is made.

5. The parameter settings for a process must be determined

    so that variation of the product response is only slight.

6. The design parameters and noise factors in orthogonal arrays are arranged so

    that computation of each experimental combination is made.

7. A multi-response signal-to-noise ratio is developed so that the optimum

    conditions in the parameter design stage can be determined.

8. Whether or not the experimental results are valid

    can not be verified by human judgement.

9. The effectiveness of the proposed method is demonstrated by analysis results.

10. Applicability of the method could be limited with insignificant t-values of the

    regression coefficient.

11. The complexity of the computational process is increased in the presence

    of the conventional method.

12. The equation is difficult to explain by Taguchi's quality loss.

13. A safety valve is contained in the machine for when cautionary measures must be taken by the inspector.

14. Evaluation of the course materials must be made by the class leader.

15. Design of the system by the engineer is allowed by the department manager.

別忘了休息一下喔！

Answers

Exercise 6

1. Operational procedures are manipulated so that the parameters can be determined.

Engineers manipulate operational procedures to determine the parameters.

2. The Taguchi method is thoroughly assessed so that the effect of various factors on performance variation can be understood.

Designers thoroughly assess the Taguchi method to understand how various factors affect its performance variation.

EDITOR'S NOTE 2.11   To increase word variety in a sentence, *various, varying, and varied* can be used as alternatives to *different* when the Chinese meaning is 不同的 .

3. The function is minimized so that suitable operating conditions are satisfied.

They minimize the function to satisfy suitable operating conditions.

EDITOR'S NOTE 2.12   To increase word variety in a sentence, *satisfy, fulfill, and adhere to* can be used instead of always saying *meet* when the Chinese meaning is 滿足 .

Similarly, depending on the sentence's context, *adequate and appropriate* can be used as alternatives to *suitable* when the Chinese meaning is 適合 .

4. The single-response problem is focused on so that a

modification of the operating system is made.

This work focuses on the single-response problem to
modify the operating system.

5. The parameter settings for a process must be determined so
that variation of the product response is only slight.

Experienced engineers must determine the parameters for
a process so that the product response varies only slightly.

EDITOR'S NOTE 2.13   Depending on the sentence's context, **slightly, negligibly, seldom,** and
barely can be used as alternatives to **little or few** when the Chinese meaning is 很少 .

6. The design parameters and noise factors in orthogonal arrays are arranged so
that computation of each experimental combination is made.

They arrange the design parameters and noise factors in orthogonal
arrays to compute each experimental combination.

7. A multi-response signal-to-noise ratio is developed so that the optimum
conditions in the parameter design stage can be determined.

This work develops a multi-response signal-to-noise ratio to determine the optimum conditions in the parameter
design stage.

8.   Whether or not the experimental results are valid can not be verified by human judgement.

Human judgement can not verify the validity of the experimental results.

9.   The effectiveness of the proposed method is demonstrated by analysis results.

Analysis results demonstrate the effectiveness of the proposed method.

> **EDITOR'S NOTE 2.14**   Although *the proposed method's effectiveness* is more direct than *the effectiveness of the proposed method*, many journals do not accept the use of apostrophes and contractions. You should double check with the journal that you are submitting to on their style usage.

10. Applicability of the method could be limited with insignificant t-values of the regression coefficient.

Insignificant t-values of the regression coefficient could limit applicability of the method.

11. The complexity of the computational process is increased in the presence of the conventional method.

The conventional method increases the complexity of the computational process.

Exercise 6

12. The equation is difficult to explain by Taguchi's quality loss.

Taguchi's quality loss has difficulty in explaining the
equation.

13. A safety valve is contained in the machine for when cautionary measures
must be taken by the inspector.

The machine contains a safety valve for when the
inspector must take cautionary measures.

14. Evaluation of the course materials must be made by the class leader.

The class leader must evaluate the course materials.

15. Design of the system by the engineer is allowed by the department manager.

The department manager allows the engineer to design
the system.

Exercise 7

Put the following sentences into active voice by using the copyediting marks on page .

1. Integration of quality loss for responses is made with the proposed method through the application of Taguchi's SN ratios.

2. The variability is reduced when the scale of the quality loss is normalized.

3. Determination of the optimal factor/level combination is made in the following procedure.

4. There is no significant effect on MRSN by any factor.

5. Guidelines in which the optimal adjustment factors in a multi-response problem are determined are presented in the above section.

6.   Necessary trade-offs should be made when choosing suitable adjustment

factors.

7.   The task in which the optimal adjustment factors are determined becomes

more complicated when multiple characteristics exist.

8.   That an adjustment factor must be found is of heavy emphasis in the

conventional scheme.

9.   There is only a slight effect on MRSN by Factor D, but a significant effect

on the average of DT-response.

10.   Six controllable factors were identified in their study.

11.   Improvement in thickness uniformity is made with the optimization procedure

proposed herein.

12.   Computation of the quality loss, determination of the multi-response signal

to noise ratio, and verfication of the experimental results are achieved by

the procedure.

13. Easy adjustment of the importance of each response can be made by the proposed procedure.

14. Conventional approaches for analysis of censored data are often difficult to be comprehended by practitioners.

15. Feasible factor/level settings are usually determined by engineers so that product quality can be enhanced.

16. Analysis of the variables is impossible by the current system.

17. Announcement of the deadline is required by the organizing committee so that sufficient time to prepare the materials is allowed.

18. Fluctuation in the speed can be performed by the experimenter so that accurate calibration of the machine is ensured.

Answers

Exercise 7

1. Integration of quality loss for responses is made with the
    proposed method through the application of Taguchi's SN
    ratios.

    The proposed method integrates quality loss for responses by
    applying Taguchi's SN ratios.

2. The variability is reduced when the scale of the quality loss is
    normalized.

    Normalizing the scale of the quality loss reduces the variability.

3. Determination of the optimal factor/level combination is
    made in the following procedure.

    The following procedure determines the optimal factor/level
    combination.

4. There is no significant effect on MRSN by any factor.

    No factor significantly affects MRSN.

5. Guidelines in which the optimal adjustment factors in a multi-response problem are determined are presented in the above section.

The above section presents guidelines for determining the optimal adjustment factors in a multi-response problem.

6. Necessary trade-offs should be made when choosing suitable adjustment factors.

Engineers should make necessary trade-offs when choosing suitable adjustment factors.

7. The task in which the optimal adjustment factors are determined becomes more complicated when multiple characteristics exist.

Multiple characteristics complicate the task of determining the optimal adjustment factors.

8. That an adjustment factor must be found is of heavy emphasis in the conventional scheme.

The conventional scheme heavily emphasizes finding an adjustment factor.

EDITOR'S NOTE 2.15   Depending on the sentence's context, ***obtaining, deriving, attaining, locating*** and ***identifying*** can be used as alternatives to ***finding*** when the Chinese meaning is 尋找 .

9. There is only a slight effect on MRSN by Factor D, but a significant effect on the average of DT-response.

Although slightly affecting MRSN, Factor D significantly affects the average of DT-response..

10. Six controllable factors were identified in their study.

Their study identified six controllable factors.

11. Improvement in thickness uniformity is made with the optimization procedure proposed herein.

The optimization procedure proposed herein improves the thickness uniformity.

EDITOR'S NOTE 2.16   To increase word variety in a sentence, ***enhances, upgrades,*** and ***elevates*** can be used instead of always saying ***improves*** when the Chinese meaning is 改善 .

12. Computation of the quality loss, determination of the multi-response signal to noise ratio, and verfication of the experimental results are achieved by the procedure.

The procedure computes the quality loss, determines the multi-response signal to noise ratio, and verifies the experimental results.

13. Easy adjustment of the importance of each response can be made by the proposed procedure.

The proposed procedure can easily adjust the importance of each response.

EDITOR'S NOTE 2.17 Depending on the sentence's context, **adjust, alter, modify,** and **vary** can be used as alternatives to **change** when the Chinese meaning is 改變 .

14. Conventional approaches for analysis of censored data are often difficult to be comprehended by practitioners.

Practitioners often have difficulty in comprehending conventional approaches for analyzing censored data.

EDITOR'S NOTE 2.18 Depending on the sentence's context, **comprehend, perceive,** and **understand** can be used as alternatives to **realize** when the Chinese meaning is 瞭解 .

Similarly, depending on the sentence's context, **elucidate** and **clarify** can be used as alternatives to **make clear** when the Chinese meaning is 弄清楚 .

15. Feasible factor/level settings are usually determined by engineers so that product quality can be enhanced.

Engineers usually determine feasible factor/level settings to enhance product quality.

16. Analysis of the variables is impossible by the current system.

The current system can not analyze the variables.

Exercise 7

17. Announcement of the deadline is required by the organizing

committee so that sufficient time to prepare the materials is

allowed.

The organizing committee must announce the deadline to
allow sufficient time to prepare the materials.

18. Fluctuation in the speed can be performed by the experimenter so

that accurate calibration of the machine is ensured.

The experimenter can fluctuate the speed to calibrate the
machine accurately.

起來走走動動吧！

Unit Three

Use Verbs Instead of Nouns

動詞代替名詞

Wordiness also comes from creating nouns out of verbs (known as nominalizations). This tendency leads to weak verbs, which will be further discussed in Unit Four. In addition, overusing nouns instead of verbs also creates needless prepositions. Consider the following examples:

句子冗贅的原因也可能是使用太多的名詞，通常這些名詞是由動詞轉化來的，而結果是使動詞更無力，此部份會在第四單元詳論。此外，過份的濫用名詞也帶來了多餘的介係詞。細想以下例句：

Original

The committee must make a consideration of the proposal.

Revised

The committee must consider the proposal.

Original

The engineer performed calibration of the machine.

Revised

The engineer calibrated the machine.

Original

The researcher conducted an experiment on the new material.

Revised

The researcher experimented with the new material.

Original

The group has to make a discovery of all feasible options.

Revised

The group must discover all feasible options.

Other examples include

give consideration to	consider
reach a conclusion	conclude
undertake an investigation of	investigate
make a provision for	provide

Exercise 8

Correct the following sentences using the copyediting marks on page *.*

1. Difficulty is encountered in explanation of the method to inexperienced engineers owing to its computational complexity.

2. Simulation of the program is performed in this study.

3. A slight increase occurs in the deposition rate

4. Knowledge of how the variables are distributed is not required by novice engineers.

5. Not only is the variability of the control factors considered by the proposed procedure, but implementation of related tasks is performed by that same procedure.

6. A recommendation of using iterative least squares (ILS) as a simple method for analysis of censored data was made by Schmee and Hahn(1990).

7.   Normalization of operations is achieved by a

     simple calculation of the scores.

8.   Improvement of the condition is achieved by variation

     of the control factors

9.   A recommendation is made here that the program be

     simulated by the engineer.

10. The operator made a reservation of the ticket for me.

11. The system performs an assignment of the weights to

     the variables.

12. The next phase performed an examination of the unknown

     factors.

13. Assessment of a student's willingness to study by an instructor

     is possible through the close examination of his or her academic

     performance.

Exercise 8

14. Solution of environmental problems is heavily dependent on responsiveness

of the local community to governmental legislation.

15. Promulgation of accurate information to the public can not be done

by conventional approaches.

站起來活動吧！
免得骨頭僵硬喔～

Answers

Exercise 8

1. Difficulty is encountered in explanation of the method to
   inexperienced engineers owing to its computational
   complexity.

   Explaining the method to inexperienced engineers is difficult owing
   to its computational complexity.

   > **EDITOR'S NOTE 3.1**   The original sentence is confusing because it is unclear who is explaining the
   > method to the inexperienced engineers. Although the revised sentence still does not reveal who is
   > explaining the method, the sentence is simplified by turning the noun (explanation) into a verb and
   > putting the action towards the front of the sentence.

2. Simulation of the program is performed in this study.

   This study simulates the program.

3. A slight increase occurs in the deposition rate.

   The deposition rate slightly increases.

   > **EDITOR'S NOTE 3.2**   Although the original sentence is in active voice, the verb (occurs) does not
   > express what the deposition rate does as clearly as the revised sentence when the noun (a slight
   > increase) is turned into a verb.

4. ~~Knowledge of~~ how the variables are distributed ~~is not required by~~ novice engineers, *do not need to*

Novice engineers do not need to know how the variables are distributed.

EDITOR'S NOTE 3.3 In addition to turning the subject (knowledge) into a verb, the revised sentence switches from passive to active voice.

5. ~~Not only is~~ the variability of the control factors considered~~by~~ *In addition to* the proposed procedure, ~~but~~ implementation of related tasks

is performed by that same procedure.

In addition to considering the variability of the control factors, the proposed procedure implements related tasks.

EDITOR'S NOTE 3.4 Depending on the sentence's context, *implement, execute, perform* and *promulgate* can be used as alternatives to *carry out* when the Chinese meaning is 執行／實行 .

6. ~~A~~ recommend~~ation of~~ *ed* using iterative least squares (ILS) as

a simple method for analy~~sis of~~ *zing* censored data ~~was made by~~

Schmee and Hahn(1990),

Schmee and Hahn (1990) recommended using iterative least squares (ILS) as a simple method for analyzing censored data.

EDITOR'S NOTE 3.5 To increase word variety in a sentence, *method, means, approach,* and *strategy* can be used instead of always saying *way* when the Chinese meaning is 方法 .

7. Normalization of operations is achieved by a simple calculation of the scores.

Simply calculating the scores normalizes operations.

EDITOR'S NOTE 3.6 Turning two nouns into verbs and switching from passive to active voice greatly simplify the sentence's meaning.

8. Improvement of the condition is achieved by variation of the control factors.

Varying the control factors improves the condition.

9. A recommendation is made here that the program be simulated by the engineer.

We recommend that the engineer simulates the program.

EDITOR'S NOTE 3.7 Although the writer should be careful not to overuse First Person (*We, I, My, Our*) in a technical document, using *We* in the revised sentence is acceptable because an opinion is being expressed. Other common First Person expressions are *We believe* , *We can infer* , *We postulate* , and *We hypothesize* .

10. The operator made a reservation of the ticket for me.

The operator reserved the ticket for me.

11. The system performs an assignment of the weights to the variables.

Exercise 8

The system assigns the weights to the variables.

12. The next phase ~~performed an examination of~~ examined the unknown

    factors.

    The next phase examined the unknown factors.

13. ~~Assessment of~~ a student's willingness to study ~~by~~ an instructor can

    ~~is possible through the close examination of~~ by closely examining his or her academic

    performance.

    An instructor can assess a student's willingness to study
    by closely examining his or her academic performance.

14. ~~Solution of~~ Solving environmental problems ~~is~~ heavily ~~dependent~~ depends on responsiveness

    how ~~of~~ the local community ~~to~~ responds to governmental legislation.

    Solving environmental problems heavily depends on how
    the local community responds to governmental legislation.

    EDITOR'S NOTE 3.8　Depending on the degree to what *solving* implies, *alleviating,*
    modifying, resolving, eliminating, and *eradicating* can be used when the Chinese meaning is
    解決 .

15. ~~Promulgation of~~ Promulgate accurate information to the public can not ~~be done~~

    by conventional approaches.

    Conventional approaches can not promulgate accurate
    information to the public.

Exercise 9

Correct the following sentences using the proofreading marks on page *.*

1.　A comparison is made of the advantages and disadvantages of the methods in this study so that an appropriate one can be selected.

2.　A thorough review of linear estimation methods was made in their investigation so that the life data could be understood.

3.　Comprehension of the maximum likelihood method is difficult for engineers with limited statistical training.

4.　Computational simplicity of linear estimation methods compared with MLE methods is apparent.

5.　Consideration of the interaction and variability of variables is not made by the conventional approach.

6.　Identification and assessment of several models is possible.

7. Promulgation and verification of the accreditation standards is

    impossible.

8. This cycle is continued with until fluctuation of the selected model stops.

9. An evaluation of their adequacy can be made with the proposed scheme.

10. Reduction of the task complexity is achieved by application of the nonparametric

    technique to industrial settings.

11. Only those factors having significant effects on the response average are

    identified by the proposed procedure so that unreplicated experiments can

    be interpreted.

12. Selection is made of the optimal levels by experienced engineers for the

    factors having significant effects on the response average and standard

    deviation.

13. A serious limitation on the effectiveness of the current system is caused

by user demand.

14. Creation of new genes is possible by innovative technologists.

15. The requirement that ID cards must be shown by students when entering the

library is stipulated by school policy.

別忘了休息一下喔！

Answers

Exercise 9

1.   A comparison is made of the advantages and disadvantages of the methods in this study so that an appropriate one can be selected.

This study compares the advantages and disadvantages
of the methods to select an appropriate one.

EDITOR'S NOTE 3.9   Turning the subject into a verb and switching two passive voice phrases into active ones greatly clarify this sentence.

2.   A thorough review of linear estimation methods was made in their investigation so that the life data could be understood.

Their investigation thoroughly reviewed linear estimation
methods to understand the life data.

3.   Comprehension of the maximum likelihood method is difficult for engineers with limited statistical training.

Engineers with limited statistical training have difficulty in
comprehending the maximum likelihood method.

4. Computational simplicity of linear estimation methods compared with MLE methods is apparent.

Linear estimation methods appear to be computationally simpler than MLE ones.

5. Consideration of the interaction and variability of variables is not made by the conventional approach.

The conventional approach does not consider the interaction and variability of variables.

EDITOR'S NOTE 3.10 To increase word variety in a sentence, *evaluate* and *assess* can be used instead of always saying *consider* when the Chinese meaning is 考慮.

6. Identification and assessment of several models is possible.

Several models can be identified and assessed.

7. Promulgation and verification of the accreditation standards is impossible.

The accreditation standards can not be promulgated or verified.

8. This cycle is continued with until fluctuation of the selected model stops.

This cycle continues until the selected model stops fluctuating.

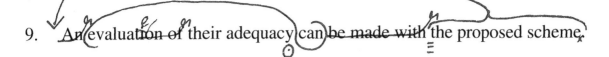

Exercise 9

9.   An evaluation of their adequacy can be made with the proposed scheme.

The proposed scheme can evaluate their adequacy.

10. Reduction of the task complexity is achieved by application of the nonparametric

technique to industrial settings.

Applying the nonparametric technique to industrial settings
reduces the task complexity.

11. Only those factors having significant effects on the response average are

identified by the proposed procedure so that unreplicated experiments can

be interpreted.

The proposed procedure identifies only those factors that
significantly affect the response average to interpret
unreplicated experiments.

12. Selection is made of the optimal levels by experienced engineers for the

factors having significant effects on the response average and standard

deviation.

Experienced engineers select the optimal levels for the
factors significantly affecting the response average and
standard deviation.

13. A serious limitation on the effectiveness of the current system is caused by user demand.

User demand seriously limits the current system's effectiveness.

14. Creation of new genes is possible by innovative technologists.

Innovative technologists can create new genes.

15. The requirement that ID cards must be shown by students when entering the library is stipulated by school policy.

School policy requires that students show their ID cards when entering the library.

EDITOR'S NOTE 3.11   Depending on the sentence's context, ***requires*** and ***stipulates*** can be used as alternatives to ***needs*** when the Chinese meaning is 需要 .

Exercise 10

Correct the following sentences using the copyediting marks on page **XIV** .

1. Introduction of the MRSN ratio is possible by integration of the quality

    loss for all responses.

2. Optimization of multi-response problems in the Taguchi method is

    achieved in this work by the procedure proposed herein.

3. Dissemination of imprecise information can not be effectively done by

    conventional MADM methods.

4. Constraints on fuzzy MADM approaches are imposed by

    cumbersome computation.

5. Conversion of fuzzy data into crisp scores is achieved in the first

    phase.

6. The fact that the attributes must be numerical and comparable is

    stipulated by TOPSIS.

7.   The relative closeness computed in TOPSIS can be used as a performance

        assessment of multi-response problems in the Taguchi method.

8.   Measurement of each response must be carefully made by the

        standard.

9.   Systematic optimization of the scheme is the focus of this section.

10. Determination from the experience of an engineer shows how

        pressure is affected by time.

11. Further analysis of the facility is necessary for the practitioner

        to make an adjustment of the parameter settings.

12. Minimization of A and B levels can be achieved by setting factors A

        and B at A2.

Answers
Exercise 10

1. ~~Introduction of~~ the MRSN ratio ~~is possible by~~ integration of the quality loss for all responses.

Integrating the quality loss for all responses can introduce
the MRSN ratio.

2. ~~Optimization of~~ multi-response problems in the Taguchi method ~~is achieved in~~ this work ~~by the~~ procedure proposed herein.

This work proposes a procedure to optimize multi-response
problems in the Taguchi method.

> ***EDITOR'S NOTE 3.12***　To increase word variety in a sentence, ***presents*** and occassionally ***describes*** can be used instead of always saying ***proposes*** when the Chinese meaning is 提出 .

3. ~~Dissemination of~~ imprecise information ~~can not be effectively~~ done by conventional MADM methods.

The classical MADM methods can not effectively disseminate
imprecise information.

> ***EDITOR'S NOTE 3.13***　Depending on the sentence's context, ***precise/imprecise*** and ***accurate/inaccurate*** can be used as alternatives to ***correct/incorrect*** when the Chinese meaning is 正確 / 不正確 .

4. Constraints on fuzzy MADM approaches are imposed by cumbersome computation.

Cumbersome computation constrains fuzzy MADM
approaches.

EDITOR'S NOTE 3.14 To increase word variety in a sentence, **cumbersome** and **complex** can be used as alternatives to **complicated** when the Chinese meaning is 複雜 .

5. Conversion of fuzzy data into crisp scores is achieved in the first phase.

The first phase converts fuzzy data into crisp scores.

6. The fact that the attributes must be numerical and comparable is stipulated by TOPSIS.

TOPSIS stipulates that the attributes must be numerical
and comparable.

7. The relative closeness computed in TOPSIS can be used as a performance assessment of multi-response problems in the Taguchi method.

The relative closeness computed in TOPSIS can assess
the performance of multi-response problems in the
Taguchi method.

8.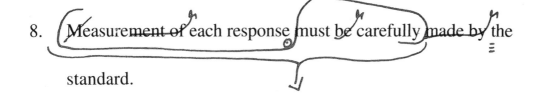
    Measurement of each response must be carefully made by the
    standard.

    The standard must carefully measure each response.

9.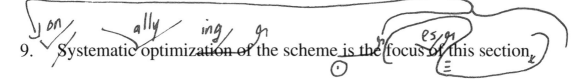
    Systematic optimization of the scheme is the focus of this section.

    This section focuses on systematically optimizing the
    scheme.

10. Determination from the experience of an engineer shows how
    pressure is affected by time.

    An engineer's experience determines how time affects
    pressure.

11. Further analysis of the facility is necessary for the practitioner
    to make an adjustment of the parameter settings.

    The practitioner must further analyze the facility to adjust
    the parameter settings.

12. Minimization of A and B levels can be achieved by setting factors A
    and B at A2.

    Setting factors A and B at A2 can minimize A and B
    levels.

Exercise 11

Correct the following sentences using the copyediting marks on page **XIV** .

1. How to adjust multiple settings of the process parameters was

    outside of the knowledge of the engineers.

2. Standardization of the accreditation procedures was

    achieved by the committee.

3. For optimization of the conditions for robust design

    problems, the applicability of a novel approach is performed

    in this study.

4. An experiment of the PCVD process in IC manufacturing

    is required of the engineer.

5. Significant contributions by the proposed procedure are

    made to the manufacturing sector.

6. Transformation of the structure is achieved by strict

    control of the variables.

7. A conclusion is made in this study that it is necessary for

    the parameters to be varied by engineers to ensure that

    operations are effectively controlled by the system.

8. An assessment of the proposed method in this section is

    made so that accurate data can be ensured.

9. Complexity of the computational process is increased by

    their approach.

10. Described in the following section is how implementation of

    the control factor is achieved by the proposed scheme.

11. No significant effect on the mean response is made by the

    factor.

12. Assessment of the product's reliability is made by the practitioner

    is achieved through means of compilation of statistics.

Answers

Exercise 11

1. How to adjust multiple settings of the process parameters was outside of the knowledge of the engineers.

The engineers did not know how to adjust multiple settings of the process parameters.

2. Standardization of the accreditation procedures was achieved by the committee.

The committee standardized the accreditation procedures.

3. For optimization of the conditions for robust design problems, the applicability of a novel approach is performed in this study.

This study applies a novel approach to optimize the conditions for robust design problems.

4. An experiment of the PCVD process in IC manufacturing is required of the engineer.

The engineer must experiment with the PCVD process in IC manufacturing.

5. Significant contributions by the proposed procedure are made to the manufacturing sector.

The proposed procedure significantly contributes to the manufacturing sector.

6. Transformation of the structure is achieved by strict control of the variables.

Strictly controlling the variables transforms the structure.

7. A conclusion is made in this study that it is necessary for the parameters to be varied by engineers to ensure that operations are effectively controlled by the system.

We conclude that engineers must vary the parameters to ensure that the system effectively controls operations.

EDITOR'S NOTE 3.15   First Person is appropriate when the author wants to emphasize his or her opimion. Other examples include **We can infer**, **We postulate**, **We recommend**, and **We hypothesize**.

8. An assessment of the proposed method in this section is made so that accurate data can be ensured.

This section assesses the proposed method to ensure accurate data.

9. ~~Complexity of~~ the computational process ~~is increased by~~ *further complicates* their approach.

Their approach further complicates the computational process.

10. ~~Described in~~ the following section *is* how ~~implementation of~~ the control factor ~~is achieved by~~ the proposed scheme *implements*.

The following section describes how the proposed scheme implements the control factor.

11. *does not* ~~No~~ significant effect on the mean response ~~is made by~~ the factor.

The factor does not significantly affect the mean response.

12. ~~Assessment~~ *es* of the product's reliability ~~is made by~~ the practitioner ~~is achieved through means~~ *by* of ~~compilation~~ *ing* of statistics.

The practitioner assesses the product's reliability by compiling statistics.

Create Strong Verbs

強有力的動詞

As shown in the previous unit, the action of a sentence can be stated more clearly when verbs are used instead of nouns. However, some verbs are weak in that they do not express a specific action. Verbs such as *is*, *are*, *was*, *were*, *has*, *give*, *make*, *come* and *take* are common examples. In contrast to using such weak verbs, a writer should use strong verbs that imply a clear action. Consider the following examples:

如前單元所示，使用動詞使句子意念表現的更清晰，然而，有些動詞讓人感覺並不強勁，無法有力闡示一個動作。動詞如 is, are, was, were, has, give, make, come, 還有 take 等都屬此類。所以， 作者應使用強有力的動詞來指明一個清楚的行為。細想以下例句：

Original
The new procedure **comes** into conflict with conventional practices.
Revised
The new procedure conflicts with conventional practices.

Original
The following equation **makes** an assumption that the constructs are valid.
Revised
The following equation assumes that the constructs are valid.

Original
The section **gives** a summary of the latest technological developments.
Revised
The section summarizes the latest technological developments.

Original
The mechanism **has** the ability to compute more efficiently than other systems.
Revised
The mechanism can compute more efficiently than other systems.

Original
The committee should **make** a decision on what to do immediately.
Revised
The committee should decide what to do immediately.

Exercise 12

Correct the following sentences using the copyediting marks on page **XIV** *.*

1. No significant difference in production occurred between the two factories.

2. The industrial output was not significantly different between the two age groups.

3. The temperature is only a little affected by fluctuation of the value.

4. An increase in parameter k causes the optimal ordering quantity to decrease.

5. The larger the TOPSIS value, the better the product quality is implied.

6. The larger the target, the higher the accuracy.

7.   The engineer must make an adjustment of the parameters so that accuracy

can be ensured.

8.   This article makes a comparison of several industrial strategies in order to

ensure market competitiveness.

9.   Modification of the process by the engineer is required so that completeness

can be ensured.

10. Networks are prevalent throughout society.

11. Network topology is a reference to how the computers are physically

attached to each other.

12. The board of directors must take action based on its authority.

Answers

Exercise 12

1. ~~No~~ significant difference in production ~~occurred between~~ the
two factories.

The two factories did not significantly differ in
production.

EDITOR'S NOTE 4.1 In addition to creating a strong verb by turning a noun (significant difference)
into a verb, the revised sentence switches from passive to active voice so that the sentence is more
effective.

2. The industrial output ~~was~~ not significantly different between
the two age groups.

The two age groups did not significantly differ in industrial
output.

EDITOR'S NOTE 4.2 The verb in the revised sentence is much stronger than in the original one.

3. The temperature is only ~~a little~~ affected by fluctuation of
the value.

Fluctuating the value only slightly affects the temperature.

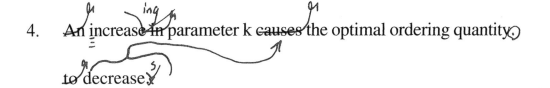

Exercise 12

4.   An increase in parameter k causes the optimal ordering quantity. to decrease.

Increasing parameter k decreases the optimal ordering
quantity.

> ***EDITOR'S NOTE 4.3*** While the original sentence is in active voice, the original verb (cause) does not
> as clearly express the action of the sentence as the revised one (decreases) does.

5.   The larger the TOPSIS value, the better the product quality. is implied.

A larger TOPSIS value implies a better product quality.

> ***EDITOR'S NOTE 4.4*** Many writers tend to use the structure in the original sentence such as ***The
> higher the A, the lower the B.*** However, the verb is not very clear. Therefore, the revised expression
> of ***A higher A implies a lower B.*** is preferred.

6.   The larger the target, the higher the accuracy.

A larger target implies a higher accuracy.

7.   The engineer must make an adjustment of the parameters so that accuracy. can be ensured.

The engineer must adjust the parameters to ensure accuracy.

> ***EDITOR'S NOTE 4.5***   Turning a noun into a verb and swiching from passive to active voice greatly
> simplify the sentence.

8. This article ~~makes a comparison of~~ several industrial strategies ~~in order~~ to

ensure market competitiveness.

This article compares several industrial strategies to ensure market
competitiveness.

> **EDITOR'S NOTE 4.6**   Unit 6 addresses how to omit needless and redundant phrases to simplify a
> sentence. One form of redundancy is putting two or more words together that express the same
> meaning. In this instance, **in order to** is a redundant phrase that can be simply expressed as **to** or **for** .

9. ~~Modification of~~ the process by the engineer ~~is required so that~~ completeness
~~can be~~ ensured.

The engineer must modify the process to ensure completeness.

10. Networks ~~are~~ prevalent throughout society.

Networks prevail throughout society.

11. Network topology ~~is a reference~~ to how the computers are physically

attached ~~to each other~~.

Network topology refers to how the computers are physically attached.

12. The board of directors must ~~take~~ action based on its authority.

The board of directors must act based on its authority.

Exercise 13

Correct the following sentences using the copyediting marks on page *.*

1. A stipulation of the agreement is that the parties are in compliance with the rules.

2. There is a general consensus among the board members that the proposal would be beneficial to the organizations.

3. The underlying notion of the proposed procedure is the assumption that all factors are equal.

4. An attempt is made in this study to minimize the total cost.

5. The proposed procedure is made up of many variables.

6. Factor A is heavily dependent on Factor B.

7. The optimization approach provides an explanation of the large-scale problem.

8. A more feasible approach makes a determination of all of the variables.

9. The following section provides recommendations on improvements to be made in the conventional design.

10. The purpose of this study is to more thoroughly understand the MCG problem.

11. There is a requirement that all factors be considered.

12. A star configuration is comprised of a series of computers connected through a central point with a device known as a hub.

Answers

Exercise 13

1.   A stipulation of the agreement is that the parties are in
     compliance with the rules.

     The agreement stipulates that the parties comply with the
     rules.

2.   There is a general consensus among the board members that the
     proposal would be beneficial to the organizations.

     The board members generally agree that the proposal
     would benefit the organizations.

     > **EDITOR'S NOTE 4.7**   Depending on the sentence's context, *correlate with, correspond to or*
     > *confer with* can be used as alternatives to *agree* when the Chinese meaning is 同意 .

3.   The underlying notion of the proposed procedure is the
     assumption that all factors are equal.

     The proposed procedure assumes that all factors are equal.

4.   An attempt is made in this study to minimize the total cost.

     This study attempts to minimize the total cost.

     > **EDITOR'S NOTE 4.8**   To increase word variety in a sentence, *attempts* and *aims* can be used
     > as alternatives to *tries* when the Chinese meaning is 嘗試 .

5. The proposed procedure ~~is made up~~ *consists (comprises)* of many variables.

The proposed procedures consists (comprises) of many variables.

6. Factor A ~~is~~ heavily dependent on Factor B.

Factor A heavily depends on Factor B.

EDITOR'S NOTE 4.9 Depending on the sentence's context, ***relies on*** and, occasionally, ***hinges on*** can be used as alternatives to ***depends on*** when the Chinese meaning is 依賴 .

7. The optimization approach ~~provides an~~ explains ~~of~~ the large-scale problem.

The optimization approach explains the large-scale problem.

8. A more feasible approach ~~makes a~~ determines ~~of~~ all of the variables.

A more feasible approach determines all of the variables.

9. The following section ~~provides~~ recommends ~~on~~ how ~~improvements to be made in~~ the conventional design.

The following section recommends how to improve the conventional design.

attempts/aims

10. ~~The purpose of~~ this study ~~is~~ to more thoroughly understand the MCG problem.

This study attempts (aims) to more thoroughly understand the MCG problem.

must

11. ~~There is a requirement that~~ all factors be considered.

All factors must be considered.

s/

12. A star configuration ~~is~~ comprised of a series of computers connected through a central point with a device known as a hub.

A star configuration comprises (consists) of a series of computers connected through a central point with a device known as a hub.

EDITOR'S NOTE 4.10   Depending on the sentence's context, stronger verbs of *consists of* and *comprises of* are preferred to *is made of* or *is comprised of* on when the Chinese meaning is 由某物製作而成 .

Exercise 14

Correct the following sentences using the copyediting marks on page *.*

1. This article is a summary of important developments in cellular manufacturing technology.

2. The guideline makes it specific that all parties will be notified by the proper authorities when a problem arises.

3. The applicant is in full compliance with accreditation standards.

4. The proposed procedure makes a provision for a robust manufacturing cell formation in a short execution time.

5. The procedure is to turn on the required machines at specified time intervals.

6. Previous literature (4) provided a formal definition of the MCG problem.

Exercise 14

7.   The different groups have to reach an agreement on how to make an

adjustment of the figures.

8.   A formal definition of what computer networking is included in

this section.

9.   An assignment of the project schedule to the site manager is made by

the foreman.

10.   An assessment of project goals is performed by the team leader.

11.   The machine operator conducts transportation of auto parts to the

assembly line.

12.   Arrangement of the assigned tasks is coordinated by the laboratory manager.

Answers

Exercise 14

1. This article ~~is a summary~~ of important developments in cellular

   manufacturing technology.

   This article summarizes important developments in cellular
   manufacturing technology.

   EDITOR'S NOTE 4.11 Depending on the sentence's context, ***critical, crucial, essential, pertinent, relevant, significant*** and ***vital*** can be used as alternatives to ***important*** when the Chinese meaning is 重要 .

2. The guideline ~~makes it~~ specific that ~~all parties~~ ~~will be notified by~~

   the proper authorities when a problem arises.

   The guideline specifies that the proper authorities will notify all
   parties when a problem arises.

3. The applicant ~~is in~~ full compliance with accreditation standards.

   The applicant fully complies with accreditation standards.

4. The proposed procedure ~~makes a provision for~~ a robust

   manufacturing cell formation in a short execution time.

   The proposed procedure provides a robust manufacturing cell
   formation in a short execution time.

Exercise 14

5.   The procedure ~~is to~~ turn on the required machines at specified time

intervals.

The procedure turns on the required machines at specified
time intervals.

6.   Previous literature (4) ~~provided a~~ formal ~~definition of~~ the MCG problem.

Previous literature (4) formally defined the MCG problem.

7.   The different groups ~~have to reach an~~ agreement on how to ~~make an~~

adjust~~ment of~~ the figures.

The different groups must agree on how to adjust the
figures.

8.   A formal ~~definition of what~~ computer networking ~~is included in~~

this section.

This section formally defines computer networking.

9.   An assign~~ment of~~ the project schedule to the site manager ~~is made by~~

the foreman.

The foreman assigns the project schedule to the site
manager.

10. An assessment of project goals is performed by the team leader.

The team leader assesses project goals.

11. The machine operator conducts transportation of auto parts to the

assembly line.

The machine operator transports auto parts to the
assembly line.

12. Arrangement of the assigned tasks is coordinated by the laboratory manager.

The laboratory manager arranges the assigned tasks.

起來走走動動吧！

Exercise 15

Correct the following sentences using the copyediting marks on page **XIV** .

1.   A laser printer normally has a higher price than an ink jet

     printer.

2.   The committee member gave a proposal that the traffic

     rules should be reviewed by the zoning commission.

3.   The technician took a measurement of the parameters so

     that the boundaries are ensured to be accurate.

4.   The focus of this study is a description of the differences

     between ink jet printers and laser printers.

5.   The members came to an agreement on how the whole issue

     should be handled by the organization.

6.   The group made a decision to let the funds be controlled

     by the treasurer.

7.   The president gave the authority to the controlling committee to

      distribute the funds.

8.   The governing body offered explanations why the law is enacted

      by the legislative branch.

9.   The investigator came up with a recommendation on a solution to the

      problem.

10.   The assessors make a verification of the product quality.

11.   The pollster regularly takes a survey of the general public on whether

      or not the incumbent should be re-elected by the constituents.

12.   The accreditation committee makes an appraisal of very qualified candidates

      that are in compliance with the standards.

Answers

Exercise 15

1. A laser printer normally ~~has a higher price~~ *costs more* than an ink jet
    printer.

    A laser printer normally costs more than an ink jet printer.

2. The committee member ~~gave a proposal~~ that the traffic
    rules should be ~~reviewed by~~ the zoning commission.

    The committee member proposed that the zoning com-
    mission should review the traffic rules.

3. The technician ~~took a measurement of~~ the parameters ~~so~~
    ~~that the boundaries are ensured to be~~ accurate.

    The technician measured the parameters to ensure accu-
    rate boundaries.

4. ~~The focus of this study is a description of the differences~~
    ~~between~~ ink jet printers and laser printers.

    This study focuses on how jet printers and laser printers
    differ.

    OR

This study describes how ink jet printers and laser printers differ.

5. The members came to an agreement on how the whole issue should be handled by the organization.

The members agreed on how the organization should handle the whole issue.

> **EDITOR'S NOTE 4.12** Depending on the sentence's context, **complete, entire** and, occasionally, **comprehensive** can be used as alternatives to **whole** when the Chinese meaning is 全部的／整個的 .

6. The group made a decision to let the funds be controlled by the treasurer.

The group decided to let the treasurer control the funds.

7. The president gave the authority to the controlling committee to distribute the funds.

The president authorized the controlling committee to distribute the funds.

8. The governing body offered explanations why the law is enacted by the legislative branch.

The governing body explained why the legislative branch enacts the law.

9.   The investigator came up with a recommendation on a solution to the

problem.

The investigator recommended how to solve the problem.

> *EDITOR'S NOTE 4.13*   Depending on the sentence's context, *obstacle, limitation, restriction,*
> *shortcoming, drawback,* and *phenomenon* can be used as alternatives to *problem* when the
> Chinese meaning is 問題 .

10.   The assessors make a verification of the product quality.

The assessors verify the product quality.

11.   The pollster regularly takes a survey of the general public on whether

or not the incumbent should be re-elected by the constituents.

The pollster regularly surveys the public on whether the
constituents should re-elect the incumbent.

12.   The accreditation committee makes an appraisal of very qualified candidates

that are in compliance with the standards.

The accreditation committee appraises very qualified candidates
that comply with the standards.

> *EDITOR'S NOTE 4.14*   To increase word variety in a sentence, *highly, rather, quite* and
> *extremely* can be used as alternatives to *very* when the Chinese meaning is 非常 .

UNIT FIVE

Avoid Overusing Sentences that Begin with *It* and *There*

避免過度使用 It 及 There 開頭句

Another form of wordiness and ambiguity is sentences beginning with ***There*** and ***It***.
使用 It 及 There 開頭的句子容易使文章語多累贅及曖昧不清。

Original
There appears to be a fluctuation in the curve.
Revised
The curve appears to fluctuate.

Original
It was her decision that led to his promotion.
Revised
She decided to promote him.

Original
There is little doubt that the proposed procedure outperforms the conventional one.
The proposed procedure undoubtedly (clearly, obviously) outperforms the conventional one.

Original
It is multifunction printers that combine printing and scanning capabilities.
Revised
Multifunction printers combine printing and scanning capabilities.

Unless ***It*** refers to a specific noun in the previous sentence, omit ***It is*** entirely.
除非 It 指的是先前句子所提特定的名詞，否則應完全地避免 It is 的句型。

Several common phrases beginning with ***It is*** can be omitted since they do not add to the sentence's meaning. Such examples include
數個由 It is 開頭的句型應去除掉，因為他們對句意並沒幫助。諸如此類的例句尚包括：

It is well known that
It may be said that
It is a fact that

It is evident that
It has been found that
It has long been known that
It goes without saying that

If omitted entirely, several common phrases beginning with *It* and
There can be stated more simply. Consider the following examples:
如果不能完全省略去除掉這種句型，則應更為精簡地描述全句。細想以下例句：

Original
It is our opinion the assumption is true.
Revised
We believe the assumption is true.

Instead of	Say
It is possible that	may, might, could
There is a need for	must, should
It is important that	must, should
It could happen that	may, might, could
There is a necessity for	must
It is necessary/critical/crucial/imperative that	must
It is noted that	Notably,
It is interesting to note that	Interestingly,
It is obvious/clear that	Obviously, / Clearly,

A simple way of omitting a phrase beginning with *It is* or *There is* is to delete that,
which, or who behind the subject. Consider the following examples:
一個簡單去掉用 It is 或 There is 開頭句型的好方法是消除在主詞之後的 that , which
,或是 or 等字。細想以下例句：

Original
It is the manager who organizes the time sheets.
Revised
The manager organizes the time sheets.

Original
There is a mechanical power that draws heat out of the combustion engine.
Revised
A mechanical power draws heat out of the combustion engine.

Exercise 16

Correct the following sentences using the copyediting marks on page .

1. It is possible that the price of a laser printer is higher than

    that of an ink jet printer.

2. There is a need for limitation of the number of users by the

    systems manager.

3. It is important that cooperation with each other be the focus

    of the study group.

4. It could happen that a decision to cancel the exhibition is

    reached by the committee.

5. There is a necessity for an agreement on the delivery terms

    by both parties.

6. It is necessary that negotiations on the final conditions be

    undertaken by both sides immediately.

7.   It is critical that consideration is made by the systems manager on the

     current status of the program.

8.   It is crucial that assessment of the control strategy be performed by

     the site manager.

9.   It is imperative that arrangement of the class schedule be done by the

     academic advisor.

10. It is not necessary for the coordination of the tasks to be the responsibility of

     the department manager.

11. There is no need for the responsibility for all of the assignments to be

     that of the team leader.

12. There is no need for corrections of the incomplete tests to be done by the

     teacher.

Answers

Exercise 16

1. ~~It is possible that the price of~~ a laser printer ~~is higher~~ than ~~that of~~ an ink jet printer.

   may cost more

   A laser printer may cost more than an ink jet printer.

2. ~~There is a need for limitation of~~ the number of users ~~by~~ the systems manager.

   must

   The systems manager must limit the number of users

3. ~~It is important that~~ cooperation with each other ~~be the focus~~ ~~of~~ the study group.

   must focus on

   The study group must focus on cooperating with each other

         OR

   The study group must cooperate with each other.

4. ~~It could happen that~~ a decision to cancel the exhibition ~~is~~ ~~reached by~~ the committee.

   may *de*

   The committee may decide to cancel the exhibition.

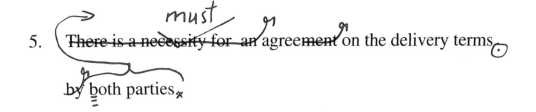

Exercise 16

5. ~~There is a necessity for~~ an agreement on the delivery terms by both parties.

Both parties must agree on the delivery terms.

6. ~~It is necessary that~~ negotiations on the final conditions be undertaken by both sides immediately.

Both sides must negotiate the final conditions immediately.

7. ~~It is critical that~~ consideration is made by the systems manager on the current status of the program.

The systems manager must consider the program's current status.

8. ~~It is crucial that~~ assessment of the control strategy be performed by the site manager.

The site manager must assess the control strategy.

9. ~~It is imperative that~~ arrangement of the class schedule be done by the academic advisor.

The academic advisor must arrange the class schedule.

10. It is not necessary for the coordination of the tasks to be the responsibility of the department manager.

The department manager does not need to be responsible for coordinating the tasks.

11. There is no need for the responsibility for all of the assignments to be that of the team leader.

The team leader does not need to be responsible for all of the assignments.

12. There is no need for corrections of the incomplete tests to be done by the teacher.

The teacher does not need to correct the incomplete tests.

Exercise 17

Correct the following sentences using the copyediting marks on page **XIV** .

1. It is necessary that a planning committee be organized.

2. It is possible that oxidation occurs during the reaction.

3. There are limitations on available options by the surrounding environment.

4. There is little research in previous literature about the inefficiency of Taguchi's two-step procedure.

5. There is little attention paid in previous literature to multi-response problems in the Taguchi Method.

6. There is more and more evidence that suggests that there is a close relation between nutrition and work performance.

7. It is important that the conflict is reduced to make a determination of the optimal setting of the design parameters

8. There is another method that employs the regression technique.

9. It is possible that the anticipated improvements are predicted under the chosen conditions.

10. There is no significant difference between the proposed procedure and Taguchi's approach in terms of effectiveness.

11. It is impossible to predict all of the unforeseeable circumstances.

12. It was a previous investigation that identified six controllable factors so that the polysilicon deposition process can be improved.

Answers

Exercise 17

Correct the following sentences using the copyediting marks on page 1.

1.   ~~It is necessary that~~ a planning committee be organized.   *must*

     A planning committee must be organized.

2.   ~~It is possible that~~ oxidation occurs during the reaction.   *might*

     Oxidation might occur during the reaction.

3.   ~~There are~~ limitations ~~on~~ available options ~~by~~ the surrounding

     environment.

     The surrounding environment limits available options.

4.   ~~There is little research in previous literature about~~ the inefficiency

     of Taguchi's two-step procedure.   *has seldom been studied*

     The inefficiency of Taguchi's two-step procedure has seldom been
     studied.

5. There is little attention paid in previous literature to multi-response problems in the Taguchi Method.

Multi-response problems in the Taguchi Method have received little attention in previous literature.

6. There is more and more evidence that suggests that there is a close relation between nutrition and work performance.

Increasing evidence suggests that nutrition and work performance are closely related.

7. It is important that the conflict is reduced to make a determination of the optimal setting of the design parameters

The conflict must be reduced to determine the optimal setting of the design parameters.

8. There is another method that employs the regression technique.

Another method employs the regression technique.

9. It is possible that the anticipated improvements are predicted under the chosen conditions.

The anticipated movements can be predicted under the chosen conditions.

10.   ~~There is no~~ significant ~~difference between~~ the proposed procedure and

Taguchi's approach in ~~terms of~~ effectiveness.

The proposed procedure and Taguchi's approach do not
significantly differ in effectiveness.

11.   ~~It is impossible to~~ predict all of the unforeseeable circumstances.

cannot be

All of the unforaeseeable circumstances can not be
predicted.

12.   ~~It was~~ a previous investigation ~~that~~ identified six controllable factors ~~so that~~

the polysilicon deposition process ~~can be~~ improved.

A previous investigation identified six controllable factors to
improve the polysilicon deposition process.

Exercise 18

Correct the following sentences using the copyediting marks on page .

1. It is important to develop a more effective approach to solve the complicated problem.

2. There were nine observations taken for each trial run.

3. There is a chance that multifunction printers include many additional utilities.

4. It is crucial that an ink jet printer is more versatile than a laser printer.

5. There can be little doubt that ink jet printers have a higher per-page cost than laser printers.

6. It is quite probable that an ink jet printer is a better choice than a laser printer if initial cost is the primary consideration.

Exercise 18

7. There is a comparison made in this article of the major differences between commercially successful keyboards.

8. It is unlikely that ink jet printers will become obsolete owing to their relatively low cost.

9. It is not necessary to train the network in all instances.

10. It is possible to configure Windows NT so that a password is required at the workstation.

11. There is an opportunity for an error to happen within the application.

12. There is a necessity for the program to be implemented by a knowledgeable systems manager.

Answers

Exercise 18

1. ~~It is important to~~ develop a more effective approach to solve the

   complicated problem.

   (handwritten: must be ... ed)

   A more effective approach must be developed to solve
   the complicated problem.

2. ~~There were~~ nine observations ~~taken for~~ each trial run.

   (handwritten: included)

   Each trial run included nine observations.

3. ~~There is a chance that~~ multifunction printers include many

   additional utilities.

   (handwritten: may)

   Multifunction printers may include many additional utilities.

4. ~~It is crucial that~~ an ink jet printer ~~is~~ more versatile than a

   laser ~~printer~~.

   (handwritten: must be / one)

   An ink jet printer must be more versatile than a laser one.

5. ~~There can be little doubt that~~ ink jet printers ~~have a higher~~

   per page cost than laser ~~printers~~.

   (handwritten: undoubtedly / more / ones)

Exercise 18

Ink jet printers undoubtedly cost more per page than laser ones.

6.   It is quite probable that an ink jet printer is a better choice
than a laser printer if initial cost is the primary consideration.

An ink jet printer is probably a better choice than a laser
one if initial cost is the primary consideration.

7.   There is a comparison made in this article of the major differences between
commercially successful keyboards.

This article compares the major differences between commercially successful keyboards.

8.   It is unlikely that ink jet printers will become obsolete owing to their
relatively low cost.

Ink jet printers will unlikely become obsolete owing to
their relatively low cost.

9.   It is not necessary to train the network in all instances.

The network does not need to be trained in all instances.

10. ~~It is possible to configure~~ Windows NT ~~so that~~ a password ~~is required~~ at

the workstation.

Windows NT can be configured to require a password at
the workstation.

11. ~~There is an opportunity for~~ an error ~~to~~ happen within the application.

An error might happen within the application.

12. ~~There is a necessity for~~ the program ~~to be~~ implemented by a knowledgeable

systems manager.

A knowledgeable systems manager must implement the
program.

Exercise 19

Correct the following sentences using the copyediting marks on page **XIV** .

1. It is important to develop a more effective approach to

    solve the complicated problem.

2. It is possible that opportunities are available for

    investment.

3. There are assumptions made by the investigator

    that the constructs are valid.

4. There is increasing evidence that supports the role of

    protein in prolonging life.

5. It is necessary to examine exactly how nutrition affects

    growth.

6. There is more and more interest in the market potential of

    carbon black in Taiwan.

7.   It is important that all alternatives be explored before reaching a

decision on what to do.

8.   There is another option that allows students to work and pursue an

academic career.

9.   There is a need for instructors to orient all incoming students.

10.   There is no significant difference between the two approaches.

站起來活動吧！
免得骨頭僵硬喔~

Answers

Exercise 19

1. It is important to develop a more effective approach to

   solve the complicated problem.

   A more effective approach must be developed to solve
   the complicated problem.

2. It is possible that opportunities are available for

   investment.

   Opportunities might be available for investment.

3. There are assumptions made by the investigator

   that the constructs are valid.

   The investigator assumes that the constructs are valid.

4. There is increasing evidence that supports the role of

   protein in prolonging life.

   Increasing evidence supports the role of protein in prolonging
   life.

5. ~~It is necessary to examine~~ exactly how nutrition affects growth.

Exactly how nutrition affects growth must be examined.

6. ~~There is more and more~~ interest in the market potential of carbon black in Taiwan.

The market potential of carbon black in Taiwan has received increasing interest.

7. ~~It is important that~~ all alternatives be explored before ~~reaching a~~ decision on what to do.

All alternatives must be explored before deciding what to do.

8. ~~There is~~ another option ~~that~~ allows students to work and pursue an academic career.

Another option allows students to work and pursue an academic career.

9. ~~There is a need for~~ instructors ~~to~~ orient all incoming students.

Instructors must orient all incoming students.

10. There is no significant difference between the two approaches.

The two approaches do not significantly differ.

别忘了休息一下喔！

UNIT SIX
Delete Redundant and Needless Phrases

其他冗詞例句包括

Many technical documents are cluttered with redundant or needless phrases that can be either deleted entirely or expressed more simply.
The writer should try to avoid needless and redundant words and phrases that only make the sentence lengthy. Consider the following sentence:

除去重複及不必要的措詞

這些擾人重複不必要的文詞其實可以完全去除，或是用更簡明的方式表達。作者若不注意這個細節則會使句子變得愈來愈長。細想以下例句：

Original
The engineer wants to take the opportunity to make an introduction of the novel property.
Revised
The engineer wants to introduce the novel property.

Other examples of wordy phrases include

Wordy	Preferred
be deficient of	lack
in a position to	can
despite the fact that	although

Another form of redundancy is putting two words together that have the same meaning. Since "rule" implies something that is "general", the writer can easily cut this phrase in half by simply saying "rule" instead of "general rule". Other examples of such phrases that can be easily cut in half to simplify the meaning include
另一種重複語句是把 2 個具同樣意義的字放在一起。例如 rule 其實就包括 general 的意思，所以千萬不要寫出 general rule 這樣的文句，用 rule 來代表就可以了。其他的例句也如法炮製如下

Instead of	Simply say
close proximity	proximity
cooperate together	cooperate
Instead of	Simply say
first priority	priority
future predictions	predictions
red colored	red
initial prototype	prototype
outside periphery	periphery
rate of speed	speed
resemble in appearance	resemble
five in number	five
adequate enough	adequate (or enough)
close proximity	proximity
first priority	priority
definite decision	decision
future plans	plans
increase in increments	increase
joint cooperation	cooperation
major breakthrough	breakthrough
most optimum	optimum
necessary requirement	requirement
rate of speed	speed
true facts	facts
very unique	unique

Exercise 20

Correct the following sentences using the copyediting marks on page *.*

1. It is well known that a majority of Taguchi method applications have

    the capacity for addressing a single-response problem.

2. It may be said that computers have the ability to incorporate

    kinds of equipment in order that the user is in a position to

    interact with the computer.

3. It is a fact that the network cards have the opportunity to be

    upgraded to meet the connection speeds in the event that the

    campus upgrades to 100Mbps hubs and routers.

4. It is evident that the college is able to make an informed decision

    through means of understanding the capabilities and cost difference

    for both 10Mbps and 100Mbps.

5. It has been found that any error that might happen will be more destructive in light of the fact that XYZ applications is in a position to make direct calls to the hardware.

6. It has long been known that the logon between the workstation and NT server is encrypted considering the fact that an eavesdropper actually wants to gain the ID and password.

7. It is our opinion that Windows 95 is for all intents and purposes a good operating system in a situation in which the user has many requirements.

8. It is possible that the error affects the necessary requirements when attempting to ascertain the location of the variables.

9. It is noted that 10Mbps network cards are basically becoming obsolete for the reason of their slow data transfer rates.

10. It is interesting to note that monitoring features in most cases inform the user provided that a performance bottleneck occurs.

11. It is the operator who makes a determination of the questions as to the phase should be implemented.

12. There is a guideline that makes a provision of the necessary requirements.

起來走走動動吧！

Answers

Exercise 20

1. ~~It is well known that a majority of~~ <u>Most</u> Taguchi method applications ~~have the capacity for~~ <u>can</u> address~~ing~~ a single-response problem.

   Most Taguchi method applications can address a single-response problem.

2. ~~It may be said that~~ computers ~~have the ability to~~ <u>can</u> incorporate ~~kinds of~~ equipment ~~in order that~~ <u>so</u> the user ~~is in a position to~~ <u>can</u> interact with the computer.

   Computers can incorporate equipment so the user can interact with the computer.

3. ~~It is a fact that~~ the network cards ~~have the opportunity to~~ <u>can</u> be upgraded to meet the connection speeds ~~in the event that~~ <u>if</u> the campus upgrades to 100Mbps hubs and routers.

   The network cards can be upgraded to meet the connection speeds if the campus upgrades to 100Mbps hubs and routers.

4. ~~It is evident that~~ the college ~~is able to~~ can make an informed decision ~~through means of~~ by understanding the capabilities and cost difference ~~for~~ of both 10Mbps and 100Mbps.

The college can make an informed decision by understanding the capabilities and cost difference of both 10Mbps and 100Mbps.

5. ~~It has been found that~~ any possible error ~~that might happen~~ will be more destructive in ~~light of the fact that~~ since XYZ applications ~~is in a position to~~ can make direct calls to the hardware.

Any possible error will be more destructive since XYZ applications can make direct calls to the hardware.

6. ~~It has long been known that~~ the logon between the workstation and NT server is encrypted ~~considering the fact that~~ because an eavesdropper ~~actually~~ wants to gain the ID and password.

The logon between the workstation and NT server is encrypted because an eavesdropper wants to gain the ID and password.

We believe

7.   ~~It is our opinion~~ that Windows 95 is ~~for all intents and purposes~~ a good

when

operating system ~~in a situation in which~~ the user has many requirements.

We believe that Windows 95 is a good operating system
when the user has many requirements.

might

8.   ~~It is possible that~~ the error affect*s* the ~~necessary~~ requirements when attempting to

find

~~ascertain the location of~~ the variables.

The error might affect the requirements when attempting
to find the variables.

9.   ~~It is noted that~~ 10Mbps network cards are ~~basically~~ becoming obsolete ~~for~~

because

~~the reason~~ of their slow data transfer rates.

10Mbps network cards are becoming obsolete because
of their slow data transfer rates

ably   *usually*

10. ~~It is interesting to~~ note ~~that~~ monitoring features ~~in most cases~~

if

inform the user ~~provided that~~ a performance bottleneck occurs.

Notably, monitoring features usually inform the user if a
performance bottleneck occurs.

11. It is the operator who makes a determination of the questions as to the phase should be implemented.

The operator determines whether to implement the phase.

12. There is a guideline that makes a provision of the necessary requirements.

A guideline provides the requirements.

Exercise 21

Correct the following sentences using the copyediting marks on page **XIV** .

1. It is important to know the pros and cons on the occasion of

    choosing a compact disk (CD) recorder.

2. There is a chance that the college will install 100Mbps cards

    notwithstanding the fact that they have served the school well in

    the past history.

3. It could happen that the college will really keep up with the changing

    times on the basis of installing 100Mbps cards.

4. To reach a decision on the manner in which to upgrade its system,

    the possibility exists for the school to replace the 10Mbps cards

    with the 100Mbps network cards.

5. It is crucial that the consumer possesses knowledge about using

    either a mouse or a track ball before making a purchase of a

    product.

6.   It is necessary that the mouse has the ability to move around the workspace in any direction in order to perform its work task.

7.   There is a need for a trackball to stay stationary under circumstances in which limited space is available

8.   It is possible that a mouse is easier for the beginning user to control for the reason that a hand is easier to move in any direction compared to a thumb.

9.   It goes without saying that it is not necessary for a trackball to have total hand and arm movement in order to move the cursor around the screen.

10.   The mouse has a sort of ball inside that basically moves along the workspace and controls electronic connections inside the particular device itself.

Exercise 21

11.   It is the board of directors who make a decision in the event that the

future plan will be accepted.

12.   There are laser printers that have a slight edge over other types of

printers in terms of printing speed and cost.

站起來活動吧！
　免得骨頭僵硬喔～

Answers

Exercise 21

1. ~~It is important to know~~ the pros and cons ~~on the occasion of~~

   must be   *when*

   choosing a compact disk (CD) recorder.

   The pros and cons must be known when choosing a compact
   disk (CD) recorder.

2. ~~There is a chance that~~ the college ~~will~~ install 100Mbps cards

   might

   although

   ~~notwithstanding the fact that~~ they have served the school well in

   the past ~~history~~.

   The college might install 100Mbps cards although they have served
   the school well in the past.

3. ~~It could happen that~~ the college ~~will really~~ keep up with ~~the~~ chang~~ing~~

   es

   by

   ~~times on the basis of~~ installing 100Mbps cards.

   The college could keep up with changes by installing 100 Mbps
   cards.

4. To ~~reach a decision on the manner in which~~ to upgrade its system,

   de *how*

   ~~the possibility exists for~~ the school ~~to~~ replace the 10Mbps cards

   may

   with the 100Mbps network cards.

Exercise 21

To decide how to upgrade its system, the school may replace the 10Mbps cards with the 100Mbps network cards.

5. ~~It is crucial that~~ the consumer ~~possesses~~ must know ~~knowledge about using~~ how to use either a mouse or a trackball before ~~making a~~ purchas~~e of~~ing a product.

The consumer must know how to use either a mouse or a trackball before purchasing a product.

6. ~~It is necessary that~~ the mouse ~~has the ability~~ must be able to move around the workspace in any direction ~~in order~~ to perform its work task.

The mouse must be able to move around the workspace in any direction to perform its task.

7. ~~There is a need for~~ a trackball ~~to~~ must stay stationary ~~under circumstances in~~ when ~~which~~ limited space is available

A trackball must stay stationary when limited space is available.

8. ~~It is possible that~~ a mouse ~~is~~ may be easier for the beginning user to control ~~for the~~ since ~~reason that~~ a hand is easier to move in any direction ~~compared to~~ than a thumb.

A mouse may be easier for the beginning user to control since a hand is easier to move in any direction than a thumb.

9. ~~It goes without saying that it is not necessary for~~ a trackball ~~to have~~ *does not require* total hand and arm movement ~~in order~~ to move the cursor around the screen.

A trackball does not require total hand and arm movement to move the cursor around the screen.

10. The mouse has a ~~sort of~~ ball inside that ~~basically~~ moves along the workspace and controls electronic connections inside the ~~particular~~ device itself.

The mouse has a ball inside that moves along the workspace and controls electronic connections inside the device itself.

11. ~~It is~~ the board of directors ~~who make a~~ *des* decision ~~in the event that~~ *if* the ~~future~~ plan will be accepted.

The board of directors decides if the plan will be accepted.

12. ~~There are~~ laser printers that have a slight edge over other types of printers in ~~terms of~~ printing speed and cost.

Laser printers have a slight edge over other types of printers in printing speed and cost.

Exercise 22

Correct the following sentences using the copyediting marks on page **XIV** .

1. It is recommended by us that the trackball be selected on
    the occasion of purchasing a user interface device of this
    type.

2. The trackball is deficient of the mobility that a mouse has
    despite the fact that the trackball requires less hand movement
    than the mouse.

3. This presentation comes to a conclusion that trackballs are at
    the present time nice to use when limited space is available
    despite the fact that not as precise movement as expected
    can be made without practice.

4. Along the lines of other browsers, Netscape Navigator has
    been proved to be great for one individual who happens to
    be working from multiple computers.

5. Netscape Navigator is also helpful if conditions are such that the users are in many cases not in close proximity to their local server.

6. The web browser in all cases gives consideration to the user's needs in a situation in which he or she is away from the office.

7. The following instructions are actually presented for the purpose of helping the e-mail user access incoming and outgoing e-mail from anywhere.

8. It is well known that a computer network serves the function of being a group of interconnected computers that cooperate together to accomplish many important tasks.

9. Computer networking is found to be a group connected together in order to share information.

Exercise 22

10. The public phone system is a good example of a network in light of the fact that it makes use of its own protocols to establish a link between two or more people that make an inquiry about the manner in which voiced information is exchanged.

11. A majority of laser printers offer a sharper and darker text print compared to other types.

12. There is a general consensus of opinion that the adopted measures are adequate enough.

Answers

Exercise 22

1.   ~~It is recommended by us that~~ the trackball ~~be~~ selected on
~~the occasion of~~ purchasing a user interface device of this

type.

(handwritten: We, when, ing)

We recommend selecting the trackball when purchasing a
user interface device of this type.

2.   The trackball ~~is deficient of~~ the mobility ~~that~~ a mouse ~~has~~
~~despite the fact that~~ the ~~trackball~~ requires less hand movement
than the ~~mouse~~.

(handwritten: lacks, of, although, former, latter)

The trackball lacks the mobility of a mouse although the former
requires less hand movement than the latter.

3.   This presentation ~~comes to a conclusion~~ that trackballs are ~~at~~
~~the present time~~ nice to use when limited space is available
~~despite the fact that not as~~ precise movement ~~as expected~~
~~can be made without practice.~~ is required to achieve

(handwritten: des, although, is required to achieve)

This presentation concludes that trackballs are nice to use when
limited space is available although practice is required to achieve
precise movement.

Exercise 22

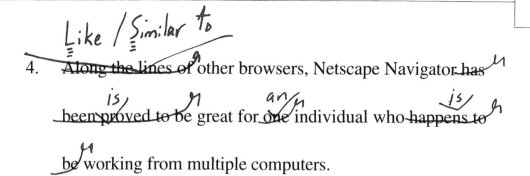

4. ~~Along the lines of~~ other browsers, Netscape Navigator ~~has~~ ~~been proved to be~~ great for ~~one~~ individual who ~~happens to~~ ~~be~~ working from multiple computers.

Like (OR Similar to) other browsers, Netscape Navigator
is great for an individual who is working from multiple
computers.

5. Netscape Navigator is also helpful if ~~conditions are such that~~ the users
are ~~in many cases~~ often not ~~in close proximity to~~ near their local server.

Netscape Navigator is also helpful if the users are often
not near their local server.

6. The web browser ~~in all cases~~ always gives consideration to the user's needs ~~in a~~ when
~~situation in which~~ he or she is away from the office.

The web browser always considers the user's needs when
he or she is away from the office.

7. The following instructions are ~~actually~~ presented ~~for the purpose of~~ to helping
the e-mail user access incoming and outgoing e-mail from anywhere.

The following instructions are presented to help the e-mail
user access incoming and outgoing e-mail from anywhere.

8. ~~It is well known that~~ a computer network ~~serves the function of being~~ a group of interconnected computers that cooperate ~~together~~ to accomplish many important tasks.

A computer network is a group of interconnected computers that cooperate to accomplish many important tasks.

9. Computer networking is ~~found to be~~ a group connected together ~~in order~~ to share information.

Computer networking is a group connected together to share information.

10. The public phone system is a good example of a network ~~in light of the fact that~~ *because* it ~~makes~~ use ~~of~~ its own protocols to ~~establish a~~ link ~~between~~ two or more people that ~~make an~~ inquiry about ~~the manner in which~~ *how* voiced information is exchanged.

The public phone system is a good example of a network because it uses it own protocols to link two or more people that inquire about (ask about) how voiced information is exchanged.

Most

11. ~~A majority of~~ laser printers ~~offer~~ a sharper and darker text ~~print compared to~~ than

other types.

Most laser printers print a sharper and darker text than
other types.

12. ~~There is~~ a ~~general~~ consensus ~~of opinion~~ is that the adopted measures are

adequate ~~enough~~.

A consensus is that the adopted measures are adequate.

Exercise 23

Correct the following sentences using the copyediting marks on page .

1. Joint cooperation between the two organizations depends on

    whether the available resources are adequate enough.

2. A major breakthrough in modern technology of today is the

    emergence of artificial intelligence.

3. The major benefit of the proposal is that the true facts about

    the very unique industrial situation can be obtained.

4. The final outcome between the two teams was an unexpected

    surprise.

5. During that period in time, the fabrics were of cheap quality

    and rough in texture.

6. The physical phenomenon that occurs in the physics field is

    often times of an uncertain condition and extreme in degree.

Exercise 23

7. The terrible tragedy was unusual in nature and of a strange type.

8. It is the terminal that communicates with the mainframe to accomplish tasks.

9. There is an engineer who adjusts the parameters.

10. It is computer networking that allows a group of interconnected computers to achieve a number of important tasks.

11. There is a manager who makes a compilation of the data and performs an arrangement of the assignments.

12. It is ink jet printers that vastly outsell laser and multifunction printers in view of the fact that they print in color as well as black and white.

Answers
Exercise 23

1. ~~Joint~~ cooperation between the two organizations depends on ~~whether the~~ (available) resources ~~are~~ (adequate) ~~enough,~~

    Cooperation between the two organizations depends on adequate available resources.

2. A ~~major~~ breakthrough in modern technology ~~of today~~ is the

    emergence of artificial intelligence.

    A breakthrough in modern technology is the emergence of artificial intelligence.

3. The major benefit of the proposal is ~~that~~ the ~~true~~ facts about *the ability to obtain*

    the very unique industrial situation ~~can be obtained,~~

    The major benefit of the proposal is the ability to obtain the facts about the unique industrial situation.

4. The ~~final~~ outcome between the two teams was an ~~unexpected~~

    surprise.

    The outcome between the two teams was a surprise.

Exercise 23

5. During that period ~~in time~~, the fabrics were ~~of~~ cheap ~~quality~~ and rough ~~in~~ texture.

   During that period, the fabrics were cheap and rough textured.

6. The physical phenomenon that occurs in ~~the~~ physics ~~field~~ is often ~~times of an~~ uncertain ~~condition~~ and extreme ~~in degree~~.

   The physical phenomenon that occurs in physics is often uncertain and extreme.

7. The ~~terrible~~ tragedy was unusual ~~in nature~~ and ~~of a~~ strange ~~type~~.

   The tragedy was unusual and strange.

8. ~~It is~~ the terminal ~~that~~ communicates with the mainframe to accomplish tasks.

   The terminal communicates with the mainframe to accomplish tasks.

9. ~~There is~~ an engineer ~~who~~ adjusts the parameters.

   An engineer adjusts the parameters.

10. ~~It is~~ computer networking ~~that~~ allows a group of interconnected
    many/several
    computers to achieve ~~a number of~~ important tasks.

    Computer networking allows a group of interconnected
    computers to achieve many (OR several) important tasks.

11. ~~There is~~ a manager ~~who makes a~~ compilation of the data and ~~performs an~~ arrange~~ment of~~ the assignments.

A manager compiles the data and arranges the assignments.

12. ~~It is~~ ink jet printers ~~that~~ vastly outsell laser and multifunction printers ~~in view of the fact that~~ *because* they print in color as well as black and white.

Ink jet printers vastly outsell laser and multifunction printers because they print in color as well as black and white.

別忘了休息一下喔！

Exercise 24

Match the unclear word or phrase with the concise one. The first one has been done for you.

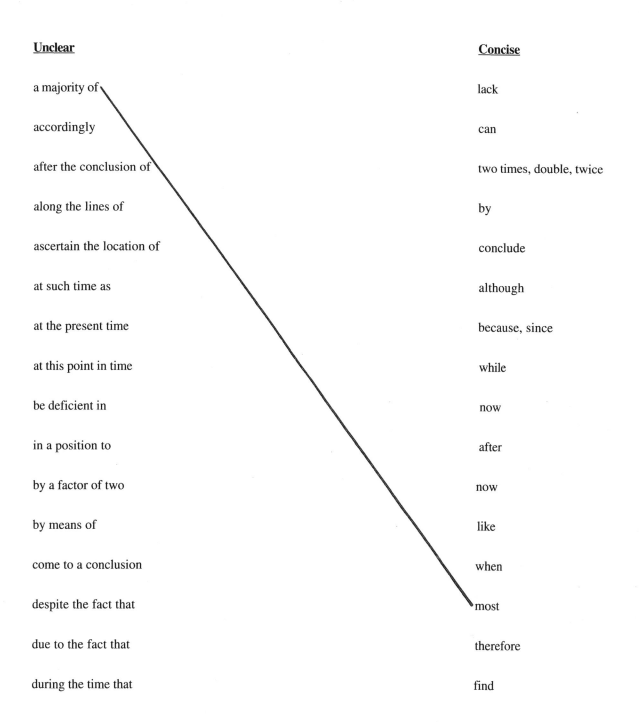

Unclear	Concise
a majority of	lack
accordingly	can
after the conclusion of	two times, double, twice
along the lines of	by
ascertain the location of	conclude
at such time as	although
at the present time	because, since
at this point in time	while
be deficient in	now
in a position to	after
by a factor of two	now
by means of	like
come to a conclusion	when
despite the fact that	most
due to the fact that	therefore
during the time that	find

Answers

Exercise 24

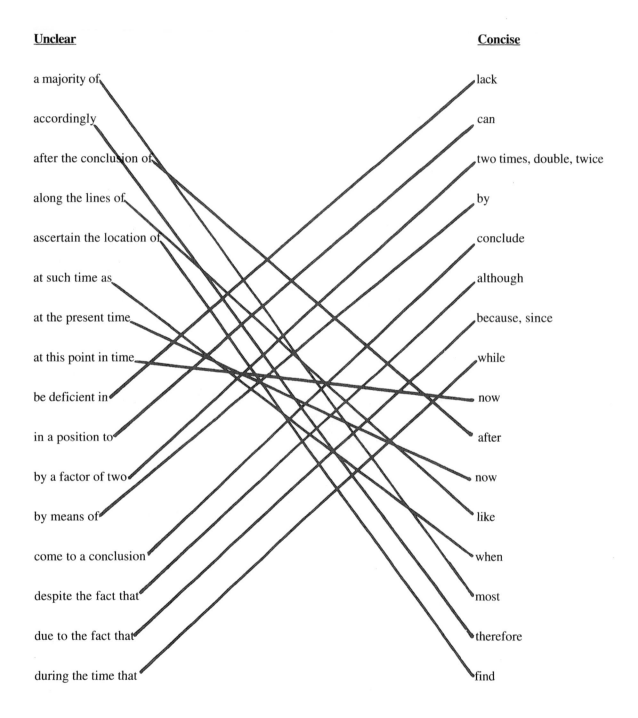

Unclear

a majority of

accordingly

after the conclusion of

along the lines of

ascertain the location of

at such time as

at the present time

at this point in time

be deficient in

in a position to

by a factor of two

by means of

come to a conclusion

despite the fact that

due to the fact that

during the time that

Concise

lack

can

two times, double, twice

by

conclude

although

because, since

while

now

after

now

like

when

most

therefore

find

Exercise 25

Match the unclear word or phrase with the concise one. The first one has been done for you.

Unclear	Concise
accordingly	largely
for the purpose of	often
for the reason that	never
for this reason	several, many
give consideration to	if
give indication of	am/is/are
happens to be	indicate/suggest
if conditions are such that	to, for
in a number of	because, since
in all cases	thus, therefore
in case	usually
in close proximity to	always
is in excess of	near
in large measure	so
in many cases	exceeds
in most cases	if
in no case	consider,examine

Answers

Exercise 25

Unclear

Concise

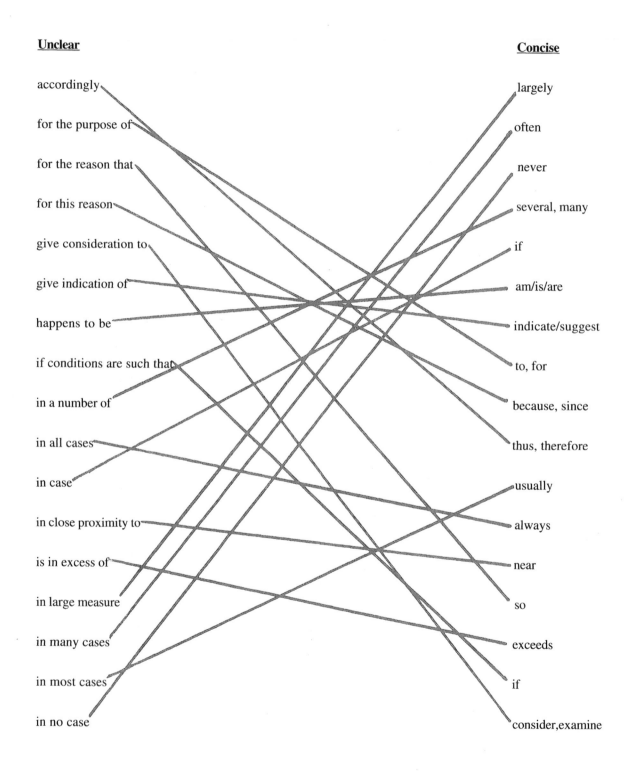

accordingly

for the purpose of

for the reason that

for this reason

give consideration to

give indication of

happens to be

if conditions are such that

in a number of

in all cases

in case

in close proximity to

is in excess of

in large measure

in many cases

in most cases

in no case

largely

often

never

several, many

if

am/is/are

indicate/suggest

to, for

because, since

thus, therefore

usually

always

near

so

exceeds

if

consider,examine

Exercise 26

Match the unclear word or phrase with the concise one. The first one has been done for you.

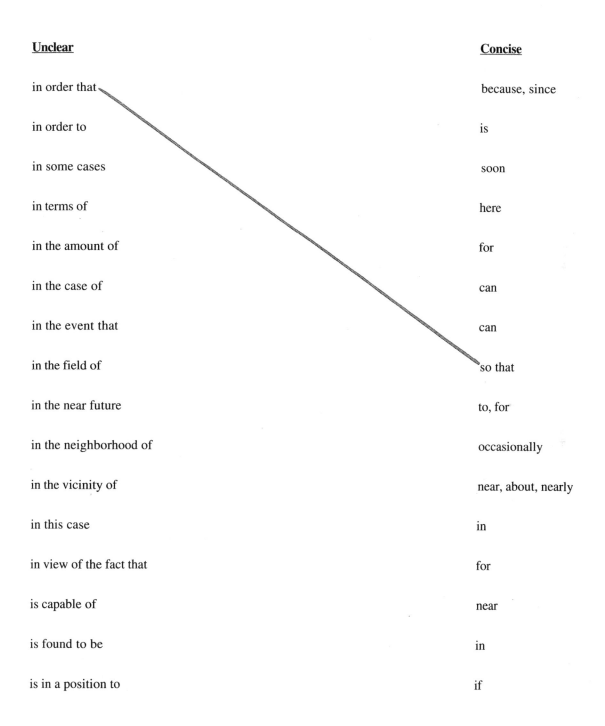

Unclear	**Concise**
in order that	because, since
in order to	is
in some cases	soon
in terms of	here
in the amount of	for
in the case of	can
in the event that	can
in the field of	so that
in the near future	to, for
in the neighborhood of	occasionally
in the vicinity of	near, about, nearly
in this case	in
in view of the fact that	for
is capable of	near
is found to be	in
is in a position to	if

Answers

Exercise 26

Unclear

Concise

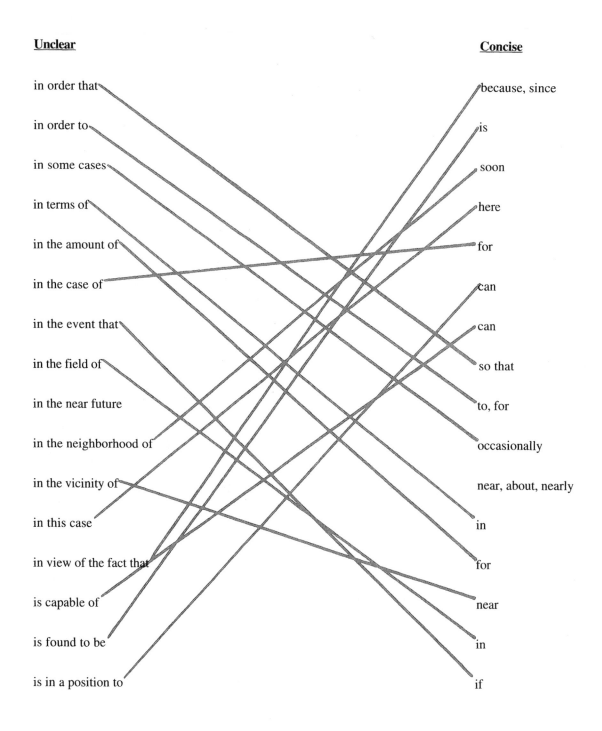

in order that

in order to

in some cases

in terms of

in the amount of

in the case of

in the event that

in the field of

in the near future

in the neighborhood of

in the vicinity of

in this case

in view of the fact that

is capable of

is found to be

is in a position to

because, since

is

soon

here

for

can

can

so that

to, for

occasionally

near, about, nearly

in

for

near

in

if

Exercise 27

Match the unclear word or phrase with the concise one. The first one has been done for you.

Unclear	**Concise**
it is noted that	end
it is interesting that	conclude
it is our opinion that	although
it is possible that	before
make inquiry regarding	interestingly
manner in which	notably
notwithstanding the fact that	we believe
on the basis of	may, might, could, can
on the order of	about, approximately
prior to	from, because, by
provided that	whether
put an end to	is
reach a conclusion	after
serves the function of	how
subsequent to	ask about, inquire about
the question as to	if

(A line connects "it is noted that" to "notably.")

Answers

Exercise 27

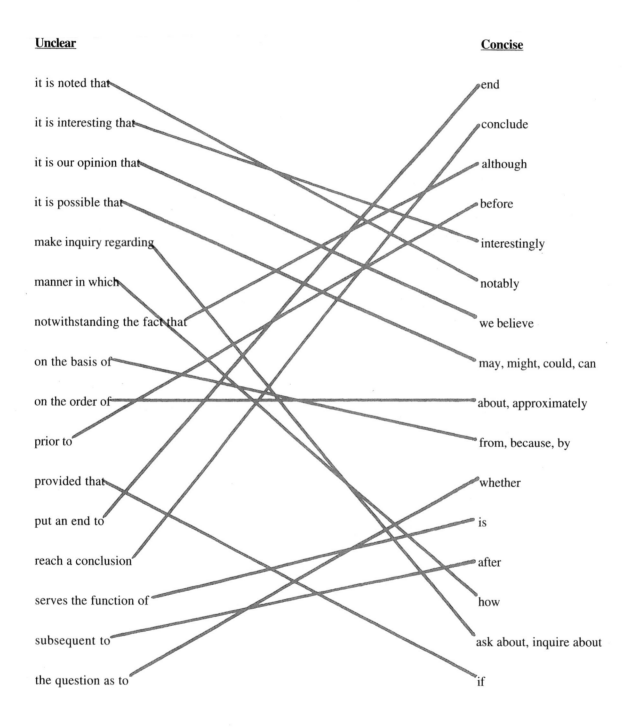

Unclear

it is noted that

it is interesting that

it is our opinion that

it is possible that

make inquiry regarding

manner in which

notwithstanding the fact that

on the basis of

on the order of

prior to

provided that

put an end to

reach a conclusion

serves the function of

subsequent to

the question as to

Concise

end

conclude

although

before

interestingly

notably

we believe

may, might, could, can

about, approximately

from, because, by

whether

is

after

how

ask about, inquire about

if

Guide to Technical Writing Curriculum

(Asynchronous Distance Learning)
at the Department of Computer Science,
National Tsing Hua University

本書同時是國立清華大學資訊工程學系非同步遠距教學科技英文寫作課程指導手冊

Syllabus

(1) Course objectives (general)

- To develop copy editing skills in a technical manuscript in terms of (a) translation errors made from Chinese to English and (b) general writing style errors.
- To organize and write the research paper in a time-efficient manner.
- To prepare the research paper for publication by meeting the expectations of one of three audiences: journal editor or reviewer, academic committee, or industrial manager.

(2) Course objectives (specific)

- What is the relation between technical writing and project time?
- What is the relation between technical writing and research design?
- How can I identify my reader's interests to make the paper more user friendly?
- How can I revise my own paper by eliminating general writing style and Chinese-English colloquial errors?

(3) Course texts

- An English Style Approach for Chinese Technical Writers by Ted Knoy Revised edition
- How to Write and Publish Engineering Papers and Reports by Herbert B. Michaelson Second Edition
- Technical Writing and Professional Communication for Nonnative Speakers of English by Thomas N. Huckin and Leslie A. Olsen International edition
- English Oral Presentations for Chinese Technical Writers by Ted Knoy
- A Correspondence Manual for Chinese Technical Writers by Ted Knoy (including computer disc)

(4) Suggested readings

●technical editing

　Substance&Style: Instruction and Practice in Copyediting by Mary Stoughton

　Style: Ten Lessons in Clarity and Grace by Joseph Williams

　Technical Editing by Lola Zook

●curriculum text

　How to Write and Publish a Scientific Paper by Robert A. Day Fourth edition

　The Scientist's Handbook for Writing Papers and Dissertations by Antoinette M.Wilkinson

　Handbook of Technical Writing by Charles T. Brusaw Fourth edition

　Technical Writing by John M. Lannon Sixth edition

　Effective Technical Communication by Anne Eisenberg

●grammatical or style reference

　The Mc-Graw Hill Style Manual: A Concise Guide for Writers and Editors Edited by
　Marie M. Longyear

　A Manual for Writers of Term Papers, Theses, and Dissertations by Kate L. Turabin Fifth
　edition

●for non-native speakers of English

　Writing Up Research: Experimental Research Report Writing for Students of English by
　Robert Weissberg and Suzanne Buker

　A Handbook for Technical Communication by Jacqueline K. Neufeld

　Principles and Techniques of English Oral Presentations: A Guidebook for Chinese
　Managerial and Technical Professionals by Chia-Jung Tsai

　Technical Contacts: Materials for developing listening and speaking skills for the student of
　technical English by Nick Brieger and Jeremy Comfort

　Learn to Listen; Listen to Learn: Advanced ESL/EFL Lecture Comprehension to Develop
　Note-taking Skills by Roni S. Lebauer

(5) Course homework

　　Written assignments will be sent for editing to the instructor via e-mail (tedaknoy@ms11.
hinet.net) as an attached file in Microsoft Word 7.0 format. The instructor will edit the files
using the editing tool inside of the "Tools" box of Microsoft Word 7.0 and, then, return to
the student. During the final week of the course, the student will submit the final assignments
on a 3.5 size diskette(Word 7.0 format).

File name	Assignment	Percent
01	Paper organization (research title, engineering / scientific objective, engineering/scientific motivation, personal motivation, outline for research, problem statement, and hypothesis statement)	5%
02	Outline for technical argument (five questions)	5%
03	Technical argument (300-450 words)	10%
04	Engineering/Scientific need (five criteria) and Problem/Hypothesis statements	10%
05	Abstract	10%
06	Introduction	10%
07	Conclusion	10%
08	Technical oral presentation of research findings NOTE: choose either general to specific or specific approach, as outlined in English Oral Presentations for Chinese Technical Writers by Ted Knoy	10%
09	Technical oral presentation (written script) (NOTE: choose one among ten options in English Oral Presentations for Chinese Technical Writers by Ted Knoy)	10%
10	Technical oral presentation (written script) (NOTE: choose one among ten options in English Oral Presentations for Chinese Technical Writers by Ted Knoy)	10%
11	Technical correspondence (NOTE: using the software package, write twelve letters by choosing from the thirty-eight options in A Correspondence Manual for Chinese Technical Writers by Ted Knoy	10%
Course grade		100%

(6) Norms for class assignments

The instructor assesses the above assignments based on the following norms:

Structure Each class assignment must adhere to the structure outlined in "Details of class assignments".

Style Each class assignment must be written in clear and concise English, free from any grammatical, general writing style, or Chinese colloquial errors.

Usability Each class assignment must not only have a particular audience in mind, but attempt to link the technical information with the particular reader's interest(s).

Details of class assignments

Assignment 1: Paper organization	
Readings:	How to Write and Publish Engineering Papers and Reports by Herbert B. Michaelson Chapters 2,4,5
Task:	**Organizing the research paper.** Organize the research paper by stating the following:

Organizing the research paper. Organize the research paper by stating the following:

- Title The title should be specific and brief, as well as easily understood to have easily identifi able keywords. Avoid long titles that begin with useless words like "Studies on," "Investiga tions on," and Observations on." Also, "A, An, or The" as title openers are also unnecessary.

- Engineering or scientific objective(s) Beginning with the word "to", list the objective(s) of your research. Common research objectives include

  1. to develop a new theory or principle
  2. to show practical applications of known principles
  3. to develop a solution for an engineering problem ina device, material, system or process
  4. to design a new structural system
  5. to develop a new or improved method
  6. to establish a set of standards

- Engineering or scientific motivations Beginning with the word "to" , list the motivations for your research. Research motivation simply means, "What is the result of obtaining my research objective?" List two kinds of motivations: (a) one that emphasizes the specific result of obtaining your objective (preferably stated in quantitative terms) and (b) anothe r that stresses the general contribution of this research. Consider this example:

  Engineering objective: (to show practical applications ofa known principle) " to apply computer simulation forcycle time control to the semi-conductor industry

  Engineering motivation: (specific) "to reduce the weakness of static analysis by 15%) and (general) "to satisfy customer's requirements by shortening wafer production cycle time."

- Personal motivation Starting out with "to", state your personal motivation for writing the paper. The most common reasons include

  to attend a conference

  to propose a new program

  to publish before competition does

  to graduate from university

Outline for research. Your engineering/scientific objectives, motivations and personal motivation affect the structure of your paper. Using the outline on page 25 of How To Write and Public Engineering Papers and Reports as an example, write an outline for your research (preferably 1 to 1 1/2 pages).

Assignment 2: Outline for technical argument	
Readings:	Technical Writing and Professional Communication for Nonnative Speakers of English by Thomas Huckin and Leslie A. Olsen International edition. Chapter 4
Task:	**Organizing the technical argument outline.** Organize a technical argument outline for your research by considering the following, as interpreted from Chapter 4(pp. 80-81) of <u>Technical Writing and Professional Communication for Nonnative Speakers of English</u>:

Technical argument

<u>Argument of fact</u>

- Subargument of existence: "Does it exist?" or "Has something happened? (Engineering/ Scientific phenomena/ event/ origin)

- Subargument of definition: "If it exists or has happened, what is it?" (Engineering/Scientific problem)

- Subargument of quality: "If it exists and has been defined, how is it to be judged?" (The range/extent/implications of the Engineering/Scientific problem) Based on the above fact, we should… (Engineering/Scientific objective)

<u>Argument of Policy</u>

- Subargument of expedience, advantage, or use: "Is the proposed activity good for the audi ence in that it is expedient, advantageous, or useful?" Engineering/Scientific motivation (specific): What are the specific results that help me obtain my Engineering/Scientific objective?

- Subargument of worth or goodness: "Is the proposed activity worthy or good in itself?" Engineering/Scientific motivation (general): What is the general contribution of this research to a particular field or area?

By applying the above model to your research, (a) write out three questions that represent your engineering/scientific phenomenon/event, your engineering/scientific problem, and the range/ extent/implications of your engineering/scientific problem; (b) using the form "Based on the above fact, we should …" write your engineering/scientific objective; and (c) write out two questions that represent the engineering/scientific motivations (general and specific) of your research.

An example can be found in

Homework sample (assignments 1, 2, 4, 5).

(NOTE: The above two subarguments in Argument of Policy should be the same as those listed as your engineering/scientific motivations in Assignment 1.

Assignment 3: Technical argument	
Readings:	Technical Writing and Professional Communication for Nonnative Speakers of English by Thomas N. Huckin and Leslie A. Olsen International edition. Chapter 4
Task:	**Writing a technical argument.** Write a technical argument (300 to 450 words) by doing the following: (a) turn the three questions from your **Argument of Fact** into three topic sentences and, then, three separate paragraphs (4-6 sentences in each paragraph); (b) use the Technical Argument sentence "Based on the above fact, we should… (Engineering / Scientific objective)" as the sole sentence of the fourth paragraph; and (c) turn the two questions from your **Argument of Policy** into two topic sentences and, then, two separate paragraphs (4-6 paragraphs).

Assignment 4: Engineering/Scientific need and Problem/Hypothesis statements	
Readings:	Technical Writing and Professional Communication for Nonnative Speakers of English by Thomas N. Huckin and Leslie A. Olsen International edition. Chapter 14
Task:	**Identifying the reader's interests (Engineering/Scientific need).** Develop a criteria formula on how to understand what the reader of your article is interested in. Consider the following adaptation from pp. 280-281 of <u>Technical Writing and Professional Communication for Nonnative Speakers of English</u>: ● Effectiveness (**Is it good?**): Is the solution effective? Will it solve the problem posed? Why? How do we know? ● Technical Feasibility (**Does it work?**): Can the solution be implemented? Does it require technology or resources that are unavailable? How do we know? ● Desirability (**Is it what we want?**): Would we want to implement the proposed solution? Does it have any undesirable effects? Does it have desirable effects? Why? What are they? ● Affordability (**Can we afford it?**): What will the solution cost to implement? To maintain? Is this cost reasonable? Is it affordable? Will it reduce costs in the future? Why? ● Preferability (**Is it better?**): Is the solution better than or preferred over any other possible solution? Why? By applying the above model to your research, write out five sentences that collectively summarize your reader's interest in the paper you want to publish. Refer to the example in **Homework samples (1, 2, 4, 5)**
Task:	**Writing the Problem statement.** Summarize the engineering / scientific problem that you are trying to solve/address (5 to 7 sentences). Refer to the example in **Homework samples (1, 2, 4, 5).** In writing the Problem statement, adhere to the following guidelines: ● State the Engineering/Scientific phenomenon/event/origin (i.e. technical argument question

	#1) in one sentence • In the next sentence, start out with the word "However," and then state the Engineering/ Scientific problem (i.e. technical argument question #2) in one sentence. • The above two steps can be combined into one sentence by using this sentence pattern: "Although (Engineering / Scientific phenomenon/event/origin), (Engineering/Scientific problem). • In the next sentence, state the range/extent/implications if such a problem exists (i.e. technical argument question#3) in one sentence. You might add an extra sentence to directly state how the problem affects the reader (i.e. reader's interests). • The final sentence should start out with the word "Therefore," and state what is needed to solve the problem (i.e. Engineering/Scientific need). Refer to the **Homework samples (1, 2, 4, 5)** for further details.
Task:	**Writing the Hypothesis statement**. Summarize your means to resolve the Engineering/Scientific problem in 5 to 7 sentences. In doing so, adhere to the following guidelines: • In the first sentence, state the Engineering / Scientific objective as if it were feasible, using the word "can". • Briefly summarize the methodology (1 to 3 sentences) used to achieve the Engineering/ Scientific objective. • State the anticipated results (i.e. Engineering motivation (specific) in one or two sentences. In the final sentence, state the general contribution of this Research (i.e. Engineering/ Scientific motivation (general).

Assignment 5: Abstract	
Readings:	How to Write and Publish and Engineering Paper and Report by Herbert B. Michaelson Second edition. Chapter 6
Task:	**Writing the Abstract.** Write the Abstract by adhering to the following guidelines: • State the Engineering /Scientific phenomenon/event/origin (i.e. technical argument question #1) in one sentence • In the next sentence, start with the word "However," and then state the Engineering/Scientific problem (i.e. technical argument question #2) in one sentence. • The above two steps can be combined into one sentence by using this sentence pattern: "Although (Engineering / Scientific phenomenon/event/origin), (Engineering/ Scientific problem). • Briefly summarize the methodology used to achieve the Engineering/Scientific objective. • State the anticipated results (i.e. Engineering motivation (specific). • In the final sentence, state the general contribution of this research (i.e. Engineering/Scientific motivation (general).

Assignment 6: Introduction	
Readings:	How to Write and Publish Engineering Papers and Reports by Herbert B. Michaelson Chapter 7 (Optional) How to Write and Publish a Scientific Paper by Robert A. Day Chapter 7
Task:	**Writing the Introduction.** Write the Introduction by adhering to the following guidelines: • State the background information(i.e. first three paragraphs of Technical argument) • Review previous attempts to solve the problem by pointing out a) the chief contributions of literature, b) the limitations of previous research and c) the Engineering/Scientific need to fill the gap. • State your Engineering/Scientific objective and describe the methodology used to attain the objective. • Describe how the results in your research satisfy the Engineering/Scientific motivations (i.e. fourth and fifth paragraphs of the Technical argument), thereby fulfilling the reader's interests (i.e. Engineering/Scientific need). In the final paragraph, list the contents of the rest of the paper.

Assignment 7: Conclusion	
Readings:	How to Write and Publish Engineering Papers and Reports by Herbert B. Michaelson. Chapter 9 (Optional) How to Write and Publish a Scientific Paper by Robert A. Day Chapter 10

Task:	**Writing the Conclusion.** Write the Conclusion for your research by adhering to the following guidelines:
	
	• Restate your Engineering/Scientific objective
	
	• Briefly summarize your methodology employed to attain the objective.
	
	• Interpret your results by asking some of the following questions:
	
	  1. Were your results expected? If not, why not?
	
	  2. What generalizations or claims are you making about your results?
	
	  3. Do your results contradict or support other experimental results?
	
	  4. Do they suggest other observations or experiments which could be done to confirm, refute, or extend your results?
	
	  5. Do your results support or contradict existing theory?
	
	  6. Do your results suggest that the existing theory needs to be modified or extended? What are they?
	
	  7. Could your results lead to any practical applications?
	
	• Stress how the results in this study confirm your Engineering /Scientific motivations (specific and general) and, ultimately, your reader's interests(i.e. Engineering/Scientific need).

2. **Developing a product or product technology (projected-oriented)** (Unit 2 of <u>English Oral Presenta tions for Chinese Technical Writers</u>). Write an oral presentation on product development from a project point of view. Adhere to the following guidelines:

- Begin the presentation by introducing the presentation title.

- Preview the topics to be covered in the presentation.

- Introduce your organization by displaying a slide of the facilities.

- Describe the missions of your organization.

- Provide the rationale for taking on the project.

- Present market data that justifies the project's feasibility

- Spell out the immediate and long term goals of the project.

- Describe the project's distinguishing features, while pointing out the strategy employed to successfully complete it.

- Conclude the presentation by pointing out the anticipated merits of the project and the positive impact that it will have.

    (NOTE: If necessary, refer to the Chinese translation of the above guidelines in Unit 2.)

3. **Developing a product or product technology (general)** (<u>Unit 3 of English Oral Present ations for Chinese Technical Writers</u>).Write an oral presentation that describes the general aspects of product development. Adhere to the following guidelines:

- Begin the presentation by directly stating its objective.

- Preview the lecture contents.

- Briefly introduce your organization, including its missions and organizational structure.

- Summarize the status of a particular product's development in Taiwan, including its market value, unique feature and characteristics, and major manufacturers.

- Mention briefly the rationale for further developing the product, along with the general course of product development.

- Highlight specific product developments made so far.

- Conclude the presentation by pointing to the future directions and challenges faced in further developing the product.

    (NOTE: If necessary, refer to the Chinese translation of the above guidelines in Unit 3.)

4. **Introducing a technology organization** (Unit 4 of <u>English Oral Presentations for Chinese Technical Writers</u>). Write an oral presentation that introduces a technology organization. Adhere to the following guidelines:

- Begin the presentation with a greetings and a preview of the presentation contents.

- Briefly overview the industry to which your organization belongs.

● Describe your organization's mission as well as highlight its historical development.

● Introduce the organizational structure.

● If necessary, outline the organization's operating funds and (for non-profit organizations) the characteristics of each funding source.

● Highlight recent technical accomplishments within the organization.

● Conclude the presentation by indicating the organization's future directions.

(NOTE: If necessary, refer to the Chinese translation of the above guidelines in Unit 4.)

5. **Introducing a research division or department** (Unit 5 of <u>English Oral Presentations for Chinese Technical Writers</u>). Write an oral presentation that describes the research division or department to which you belong. Adhere to the following guidelines:

● Start out with a greetings and a preview of the presentation contents.

● Describe the setting of your division or department within the larger organization.

● Highlight the organizational structure of the division or department.

● Point out the staff's strengths and educational backgrounds/ work experience in a particular field.

● Spell out the missions of the division or department.

● Elaborate on the manufacturing or research capabilities within the division or department.

● List the technical services (e.g. industrial and consultancy) that the department or division offers.

● Encourage the audience to think of ways to cooperate with the division or department.

● Conclude the presentation by indicating the development strategy of the division or department.

(NOTE: If necessary, refer to the Chinese translation of the above guidelines in Unit 5.)

6. **Introducing a technology** (Unit 6 of <u>English Oral Presentations for Chinese Technical Writers</u>). Write an oral presentation that describes the technological developments within your field. Adhere to the following guidelines:

● Start out by stating the objectives of the presentation and preview the topics to be covered.

● Briefly explain the factors(internal and external) that influence development of this technology in Taiwan.

● Point out the unique characteristics of this technology development in Taiwan.

● List the objectives of how to further develop this technology.

● Define the role of this technology in relation to environmental, manufacturing or technology problems.

- Briefly summarize previous efforts to solve or alleviate above problems, along with the contri butions and limitations of such efforts.

- List applications of this technology made so far, highlighting any particular characteristics or features that are unique to Taiwan's circumstances.

- Cite specific cases of such applications.

- Highlight the available opportunities for investment and cooperation in this technology market.

- Conclude the presentation by indicating future challenges in continuously applying this technology.

(NOTE: if necessary, refer to the Chinese translation of the above guidelines in Unit 6.)

7. **Introducing an industry** (Unit 7 of <u>English Oral Presentations for Chinese Technical Writers</u>). Write an oral presentation that introduces the status of the local industry to which either your research focuses on or your company / organization belongs to. Adhere to the following guidelines:

- Begin the presentation by previewing the topics to be covered.

- Briefly highlight the general characteristics of this industry in Taiwan.

- Point out the difficulties encountered in industrial development.

- Describe current activities of the particular industrial sector.

- Elaborate on the available technologies that are employed by the industry.

- Discuss the related research and development facilities in Taiwan, and how they assist/ collaborate with that particular industry.

- Outline the major research and development programs that are currently underway within the industry.

- Provide a case example of industrial development.

- Concluding the presentation by point toward future development trends within the industry.

(NOTE: If necessary, refer to the Chinese translation of above guidelines in Unit 7.)

8. **Reviewing or summarizing a technological development** (Unit 8 of <u>English Oral Presentations for Chinese Technical Writers</u>). Write an oral presentation that reviews the previous development of some technical aspect. Adhere to the following guidelines:

- Start out by previewing the topics to be covered.

- Provide a general definition of the topic that is to be reviewed, e.g. technology transfer.

- Briefly explain Taiwan's relation with that topic.

- Outline the history of industrial, manufacturing or technology development in relation to the topic.

● Compare Taiwan with other countries in terms of the topic.

● Elaborate on the research and development system in relation to the topic.

● Highlight various models or concepts related to the topic.

● Provide an illustrative example related to the topic.

● Having reviewed the topic, conclude by pointing out some of the general implications that can be made for future action.

(NOTE: If necessary, refer to the Chinese translation of above guidelines in Unit 8.)

9. **Visiting an overseas company** (Unit 9 of <u>English Oral Presentations for Chinese Technical Writers</u>). Write a brief oral presentation that is to be made when visiting an overseas company. Adhere to the following guidelines

● Start out by directly stating the objectives of the company visit.

● Introduce your organization in terms of its missions, range of research or manufacturing projects, as well as unique features or characteristics.

● Cite a specific product technology application in your organization (including future research trends).

● Conclude the talk by calling for further collaborative ties between your two organizations.

(NOTE: If necessary, refer to the Chinese translation of above guidelines in Unit 9.)

10. **Reporting on research or technical capabilities** (Unit 10 of <u>English Oral Presentations for Chinese Technical Writers</u>) Write an oral presentation that describes the current status of research or technical capabilities of your laboratory. Adhere to the following guidelines:

● Starting out by identifying the lecture's objective and, then, preview the topics to be covered.

● Describe your organization in terms of a brief history, its missions, staff, operating funds, and organizational structure.

● Describe the capabilities of experiments in your research focus, while elaborating on equipment and the kinds of experiments which can be performed.

● Introduce the main equipment in your laboratory, along with specific experiments which can be performed.

● Touch on the related hardware or software available to your laboratory.

● Inform what technical or industrial services are provided by your laboratory.

● Conclude the presentation by pointing to future directions on how research and technical capabilities can be expanded, or what potential research areas are to be explored.

(NOTE: If necessary, refer to the Chinese translation of above guidelines in Unit 10.)

Assignment 11:Technical correspondence	
Readings:	A Correspondence Manual for Chinese Technical Writers by Ted Knoy Units 1 thru 5
Task:	Task: Using the accompanying software package, write twelve letters by selecting from the following thirty-nine options. Write at least two letters from each of the following categories: (I.) Technical cooperation, (II.) Technical visits overseas, (III.) Technical visits from abroad, (IV.) Technical training, and (V.) Requesting information. **(I) Technical cooperation** 1. **Proposing information exchange**. Using 1.1 in the accompanying software as a model, write a letter proposing an information exchange with another organization. Be sure to adhere to the following guidelines: ● Refer to previous correspondence, if any. ● Directly propose an information exchange between your two organizations. ● Give background information on your organization, including objectives, major activities, and achievement. ● Welcome and/or provide suggestions regarding how to initiate the information exchange, e.g. a technical talk. 2. **Proposing information exchange**. Using 1.3 in the accompanying software as a model, write a letter proposing an information exchange with another organization. Be sure to adhere to the following guidelines: ● Refer to previous correspondence, if any. ● Introduce the major programs or activities within your department or laboratory. ● Acknowledge the achievements of the reader's corporation/organization and propose an information exchange relationship. 3. **Seeking a technology licensor**. Using 1.5 in the accompanying software as a model, write a letter seeking a licensor of a technology that your organization would like touse or to introduce to other companies in Taiwan. Be sure to adhere to the following guidelines: ● State your intention to license a particular technology. ● Briefly describe your interest in the technology. ● Clarify the role of your organization in this proposed technology licensing agreement. 4. **Seeking a technology licensor**. Using 1.6 in the accompanying software as a model, write a letter seeking a licensor of a technology that your organization would like to use or to introduce to the local industrial sector. Be sure to adhere to the following guidelines:

- Refer to your organization's previous relationship with the company.

- Describe your current project and your interest in a technology transfer from abroad.

- Commend the reader's company on its reputation for developing such products.

5. **Transferring a technology**. Using 1.7 in the accompanyingsoftware as a model, write a letter expressing the desire toexpedite the licensing of a foreign-owned technology to a company in Taiwan. Be sure to adhere to the following guidelines:

- Acknowledge their previous correspondence and commend their interest in licensing the technology.

- Clarify the role of your organization in this technology transfer.

- Request further information and offer your assistance as a facilitator.

6. **Introducing company for technology transfer.** Using 1.9 in the accompanying software as a model, write a letter introducing a company that is interested in receiving technology from abroad. Be sure to adhere to the following guidelines:

- State that a company has been located for possible technology transfer.

- Mention that the primary features, major products, and achievements of this company.

- Highlight the manufacturing or research capabilities of this company in relation to potential technology developments in Taiwan.

- Mention that you've included other information in an attachment.

7. **Seeking technical cooperation**. Using 1.11 in the accompanying software as an example, write a letter seeking technical cooperation with a company overseas. Be sure to adhere to the following guidelines:

- Mentioned who referred you to their company and state your interest in technical cooperation.

- Briefly describe your organization and its' primary objectives.

- Introduce your program and the major items to be developed.

8. **Seeking technical cooperation**. Using 1.13 in the accompanying software as an example, write a letter seeking technical coopertion with an overseas company. Be sure to adhere to the following guidelines:

- State how you heard of their company, and express your confidence in the outcome of the technical cooperation.

- Request further literature or audiovisual information regarding the company's manufacturing capabilities, along with a list of companies who have used their products.

- Briefly introduce your organization and describe its interest in intentions of technical cooperation.

9. **Proposing a framework for technical cooperation**. Using 1.15 in the accompanying soft ware as a model, write a letter proposing a framework for technical cooperation between your organization and an overseas firm. Create an illustration similar to that in 1.15 to visually clarify the relationship.

10. **Spelling out the specifics of technical collaboration**. Using 1.16 in the accompanying soft ware as an example, write a letter focusing on the details of a cooperative relationship. Be sure to adhere to the following guidelines:

- Provide a brief argument in favor of a cooperative relationship between your two organiztions. Emphasize your organization's commitment to the development of this technology in Taiwan.

- Outline the tasks that both organizations must perform to achieve successful technical cooperation (or strategy alliance).

- Request clarification in any matters concerning the cooperative agreement that remain unclear.

11. **Applying for international membership**. Using 1.17 in the accompanying software as a model, on behalf of your organization, apply for membership into an international body. Be sure to adhere to the following guidelines:

- Point our who referred or nominated you for membership into the international body in question.

- Briefly describe your organization, including objectives, major projects and achievements.

- State the purpose of your application for membership into this international body, and request application materials.

12. **Describing organizational activity**. Using 1.19 in the accompanying software as a model, write a letter describing a current organizational activity. Be sure to adhere to the following guidelines:

- Comment on the inquirer's inteest in the activity and/or objectives that your two organizations share.

- Describe any major developments or milestones in the promotion of the activity, e.g. data bank, newsletter, programs. Be sure to include the objectives of such activities or programs.

- Include the names and curriculum vitae of people who can provide further information.

13. **Reporting current activities**. Using 1.20 in the accompanying software as a model, write a letter reporting the current status of an activity your organization is involved with. Be sure to adhere to the following guidelines:

- Briefly describe the background of this activity with respect to the difficulties encountered in developing such an activity.

- Propose the solutions or steps to be taken to eliminate/alleviate such difficulties.

- State your organization's need to upgrade the level of this activity.

14. **Describing current activities**. Using 1.21 in the accompanying software as a model, write a letter describing the current status of a particular activity in your organization.Be sure to adhere to the following guidelines:

- Give a brief description of your organization, including its objectives.

- Describe your organization's involvement in a particular activity.

- Point to areas of expected involvement in the future.

(II) Technical visit overseas

15. **Proposing a technical visit (product development)**. Using 2.1 in the accompanying software as a model, write a letter that proposes a technical visit regarding product development. Be sure to adhere to the following guidelines:

- Refer to any previous correspondence.

- Mention and briefly describe any attached information.

- Commend their organization on achievements in product development.

- Explain current product development at your organization(or in Taiwan).

- Propose a technical visit and mention preliminary details.

16. **Proposing a technical visit (program development)**. Using 2.2 in the accompanying software as a model, write a letter that proposes a technical visit regarding program development. Be sure to adhere to the following guidelines:

- Refer to any previous correspondence or contact.

- Introduce your organization's program (e.g. objectives, services, and successes)

- Stress the global scope of the program and the need for cooperation.

- Propose a technical visit.

17. **Proposing a technical visit (laboratory development)**. Using 2.3 in the accompanying software as a model, write a letter that proposes a technical visit regarding laboratory development. Be sure to adhere to the following guidelines:

- Describe your position and role in the laboratory development at your organization.

- Mention who recommended you to visit their organization and why they made the recommendation.

- Emphasize that this visit is the beginning of a cooperative relationship.

18. **Proposing a technical visit (technology development)**. Using 2.4 in the accompanying software as a model, write a letter that proposes a technical visit regarding development of a particular technology. Be sure to adhere to the followingguidelines:

- Refer to any previous correspondence or contact.

- Propose a technical visit.

- Describe how this visit can meet your organization's current need to further develop a certain technology.

19. **Proposing a technical visit (technology development).** Using 2.5 in the accompanying software as a model, write a letter that proposes a technical visit regarding technology development. Be sure to adhere to the following guidelines:

- Mention who suggested that you to visit the company.

- Commend the company on development of a particular technology.

- Describe your role in developing a particular technology at your organization.

- Express your intentions for future collaboration.

- Mention any scheduling constraints.

20. **Following up on request for technical visit**. Using 2.8 in the accompanying software as a modle, write a letter reminding a company of your interest in making a technical visit. Be sure to adhere to the following guidelines:

- Refer to previous conversation(s) and circumstances regarding the technical visit.

- Restate, in a clear manner, the purpose and objectives of the visit.

- Politely refer to the lapse in time since the previous conversation, and offer to provide extra information, if necessary.

21. **Changing the itinerary of a technical visit.** Using 2.10 in the accompanying software as a model, write a letter that suggests changes in an itinerary for a technical visit. Be sure to adhere to the following guidelines:

- Commend the organization for preparations made so far.

- Explain the reason why the changes need to be made.

- State, in detail, what kind of changes should be made.

- If necessary, apologize for any unforseeable inconvenience caused by the schedule change.

(III) Technical visits from abroad

22. **Inviting a speaker**. Using 3.1 in the accompanying software as a model, write a letter inviting a speaker to participate in an event, such as a symposium. Be sure to adhere to thefollowing guidelines:

- Invite the speaker.

- State the place and time of the event, along with general topic of the lecture.

● Mention airfare and accomodation arrangements.

● Ask the speaker to provide a lecture title, handouts, and a curriculum vitae.

● Close with an optimistic appraisal of the speaker's contribution to the event.

23. **Inviting a consultant or guest worker**. Using 3.6 on the accompanying software as a model, write a letter inviting a consultant or guest worker to your organization. Be sure to adhere to the following guidelines:

● Restate the commitment to foster technical cooperation between your two organizations.

● Invite the reader to act as a consultant or guest worker.

● Propose the topics to be covered by the consultant or guest worker.

● Briefly mention financial arrangements.

24. **Proposing a technical visit's agenda**. Using 3.8 on the accompanying software as a model, write a letter proposing an agenda for a technical visit. Be sure to adhere to the following guidelines:

● State your role in the upcoming technical visit.

● Propose topics of discussion.

● Invite suggestions regarding the proposed agenda.

25. **Introducing the program for a technical meeting**. Using 3.13 on the accompanying software as a model, write a letter introducing the program for a symposium. Be sure to adhere to the following guidelines:

● Give specifics of the symposium, i.e. date, place, and time of lecture.

● Request all necessary materials, e.g. curriculum vitae, lecture topics, and complete papers

● Outline what your organization will provide, e.g. round-trip airfare, hotel accomodations, and living expenses.

26. **Providing final details of a technical lecture**. Using 3.14 on the accompanying software as a model, write a letter to provide the final details of a symposium lecture. Be sure to adhere to the following guidelines:

● Acknowledge receipt of previously requested materials.

● Mention incidentals related to the symposium lecture, e.g. translators, handouts, and transparencies.

● Restate arrangements for compensating the lecturer's expenses.

● Include a copy of the symposium agenda.

27. **Accepting an invitation for a technical visit**. Using 3.15 on the accompanying software as a model, write a letter of acceptance for a technical visit. Be sure to adhere to the following guidelines:

- State the approval of the application.

- Mention specifics, e.g. accomodations, living expenses, and additional information required.

- Propose topics of discussion.

(IV) Technical training

28. **Applying for guest worker position**. Using 4.1 on the accompanying software as a model, apply for a guest worker position at an institute or company. Be sure to adhere to the following guidelines:

- State what organization you belong to and describe your current position and background.

- Describe your current work and tell how it relates to your laboratory's development.

- State how their organization can meet your organization's need.

- Propose your stay as a guest worker and tell what your work at their organization would entail.

- Explain who will compensate for your expenses.

- Offer references.

29. **Applying for guest worker position**. Using 4.2 on the accompany software as a model, apply for a guest worker position at an institute or company. Be sure to adhere to the following guidelines:

- Briefly describe one of your laboratory's current projects in and explain how a guest worker position would greatly benefit this project.

- Introduce your organization and highlight some of your own personal research interests.

- Propose the time period for the guest worker arrangement.

30. **Applying for guest worker position**. Using 4.4 on the accompanying software as a model, apply for the position of a guest worker. Be sure to adhere to the following guidelines:

- Commend the organization on their reputation.

- Introduce the organization you are to be sponsored by.

- Briefly summarize your educational background and professional experience. State your topics of interest.

31. **Making suggestions for training curriculum**. Using 4.6 on the accompanying software as a model, write a letter suggesting the curriculum for an upcoming training session.Be sure to adhere to the following guidelines:

- Refer to a previous discussion regarding a training course on a particular technology.

- Emphasize your organization's commitment to developing this technology, along with related activities currently underway.

- Propose certain topics to be discussed during the training while giving the speaker the freedom to modify or expand on any of the proposed topics.

(V) Requesting information

32. **Requesting program information**. Using 5.1 on the accompanying software as a model, write a letter requesting program information. Be sure to adhere to the following guidelines:

- Introduce your organization and refer to any previous correspondence.

- Compare the similar objectives of your two organizations.

- Request program information and raise the possibility of future collaboration.

33. **Requesting company information**. Using 5.2 on the accompanying software as a model, write a letter requesting company information. Be sure to adhere to the following guidelines:

- Refer to any previous correspondence.

- Request a listing of manufacturers of a particular technology.

- Request other pertinent literature information.

34. **Requesting product information**. Using 5.4 on the accompanying software as a model, write a letter requesting product information. Be sure to adhere to the following guidelines:

- Describe one of your organization's current projects and explain the need for certain products.

- List the products needed. Provide as much detail as possible.

- Request pertinent information, e.g. catalogues, price lists, and sales agent information.

35. **Responding to inquiry form**. Find an application inquiry form similar to that in 5.7. Write an appropriate response to that inquiry.

36. **Requesting technology information**. Using 5.10 on the accompanying software as a model, write a letter requesting technology information. Be sure to adhere to the following guidelines:

- Mention who referred you or how you found out about the company's expertise.

- Briefly introduce your company or organization.

- Request technology information and, if possible, product samples.

- State why your company wishes to develop this technology.

36. **Requesting technology information**. Using 5.10 on the accompanying software as a model, write a letter requesting technology information. Be sure to adhere to the following guidelines:

- Mention who referred you or how you found out about the company's expertise.

- Briefly introduce your company or organization.

- Request technology information and, if possible, product samples.

- State why your company wishes to develop this technology.

37. **Requesting specific information**. Using 5.13 on the accompanying software as a model, write a letter requesting specific information. Be sure to adhere to the following guidelines:

- Directly request the information.

- Introduce your organization, and cite your objectives, major work, and achievements.

- Provide a brief background on Taiwan's relevant circumstances, as related to the need to develop the technology in question.

- Suggest the possibility of future cooperation, e.g. visits, symposiums, and technology consultation activities.

38. **Requesting technical information**. Using 5.15 on the accompanying software as a model, write a letter to request information. Be sure to adhere to the following guidelines:

- Refer to previous contact, if any.

- Mention a previous article or paper written by the reader in which you have a particular interest.

- Request information related to a specific topic.

39. **Requesting a price quotation**. Using 5.17 on the accompanying software as a model, request a price quotation for a product. Be sure to adhere to the following guidelines:

- Refer to previous correspondence, if any.

- Describe your organization's interest in this product.

- Request a price quotation for a particular product.

   Propose a next step that could be taken after the price quotation is agreed upon.

About the Author

Born on his father's birthday (September 20, 1965), Ted Knoy received a Bachelor of Arts in History at Franklin College of Indiana (Franklin, Indiana) and a Masters of Public Administration at American International College (Springfield, Massachusetts). Having conducted research and independent study in South Africa, India, Nicaragua, and Switzerland, he has lived in Taiwan since 1989.

An associate researcher at Union Chemical Laboratories (Industrial Technology Research Institute), Ted is also a technical writing instructor at the Department of Computer Science, National Tsing Hua University as well as the Institute of Information Management and the Department of Communications Engineering, National Chiao Tung University. He is also the English editor of several technical and medical journals in Taiwan.

Ted is author of the Chinese Technical Writers Series, which includes <u>An English Style Approach for Chinese Technical Writers</u>, <u>English Oral Presentations for Chinese Technical Writers</u>, <u>A Correspondence Manual for Chinese Technical Writers</u>, and <u>An Editing Workbook for Chinese Technical Writers</u>.

Ted created and coordinates the Chinese Only (On-line Writing Lab) at http://mx.nthu.edu.tw/~tedknoy

Acknowledgments

Professors Su Chao-Ton and Tong Lee-Eeng of the Department of Industrial Management at Chiao Tung University are appreciated for the use of their materials. Seamus Harris and Scott Vokey are also appreciated for reviewing this workbook.

科技英文寫作系列之一

精通科技論文(報告)寫作之捷徑

An English Style Approach For Chinese Technical Writers

(修訂版)

作者: 柯泰德 (Ted Knoy)

使用直接而流利的英文會話
讓您所寫的英文科技論文很容易被了解
提供不同形式的句型供您參考利用
比較中英句子結構之異同
利用介系詞片語將二個句子連接在一起

萬其超—李國鼎科技發展基金會秘書長

本書是多年實務經驗和專注力之結晶,因此是一本坊間少見而極具實用價值的書。

陳文華—國立清華大學工學院院長

中國人使用英文寫作時,語法上常會犯錯,本書提供了很好的實例示範,對於科技論文寫作有相當參考價值。

徐　章—工業技術研究院量測中心主任

這是一個讓初學英文寫作的人,能夠先由不犯寫作的錯誤開始再根據書中的步驟逐步學習提升寫作能力的好工具, 此書的內容及解說方式使讀者也可以無師自通,藉由自修的方式學習進步,但是更重要的是它雖然是一本好書,當您學會了書中的許多技巧,如果您還想要更進步,那麼基本原則還是要常常練習,才能發揮書中的精髓。

Kathleen Ford, English Editor, Proceedings(Life Science Divison), National Science Council

The Chinese Technical Writers Series is valuable for anyone involved with creating scientific documentation.

特　　價　新台幣 250 元
劃　　撥　19419482　清蔚科技股份有限公司
線上訂購　四方書網　www.4book.com.tw
發 行 所　華香園出版社　印行

作好英語會議簡報
English Oral Presentations for Chinese Technical Writers
A Case Study Approach

作者： 柯泰德（Ted Knoy）

內容簡介

本書共分十二個單元，涵括產品開發、組織、部門、科技、及產業的介紹、科技背景、公司訪問、研究能力及論文之發表等，每一單元提供不同型態的科技口頭簡報範例，以進行英文口頭簡報的寫作及表達練習，是一本非常實用的著作。

李鍾熙—工業技術研究院化學工業研究所所長

一個成功的科技簡報，就是使演講流暢，用簡單直接的方法、清楚表達內容。本書提供一個創新的方法(途徑)，給組織每一成員做為借鏡，得以自行準備口頭簡報。利用本書這套有系統的方法加以練習，將必然使您信心備增，簡報更加順利成功。

薛敬和—IUPAC 台北國際高分子研討會執行長
國立清華大學教授

本書以個案方式介紹各英文會議簡報之執行方式，深入簡出，為邁入實用狀況的最佳參考書籍。

沙晉康—清華大學化學研究所所長
第十五屆國際雜環化學會議主席

本書介紹英文簡報的格式，值得國人參考。今天在學術或工商界與外國接觸來往均日益增多，我們應加強表達的技巧，尤其是英文的簡報應具有很高的專業手準。本書做為一個很好的範例。

張俊彥—國立交通大學電機資訊學院教授兼院長

針對中國學生協助他們寫好英文的國際論文和參加國際會議如何以英語演講、內容切中要害特別推薦。

特　　價　新台幣250元
劃　　撥　19419482　清蔚科技股份有限公司
線上訂購　四方書網　www.4book.com.tw
發 行 所　華香園出版社　印行

英文信函參考手冊

A Correspondence Manual for Chinese Technical Writers

作者： 柯泰德（Ted Knoy）

內容簡介

本書期望成爲從事專業管理與科技之中國人，在國際場合上溝通交流時之參考指導書籍。本書所提供的書信範例（ 附磁碟片），可爲您撰述信件時的參考範本。更實際的是，本書如同一「寫作計畫小組」，能因應特定場合（ 狀況 ） 撰寫出所需要的信函。

總統府資政—李國鼎先生

我國科技人員在國際場合溝通表達之機會急遽增加，希望大家都來重視英文說寫之能力。

羅明哲—國立中興大學教務長

一份表達精準且適切的英文信函，在國際間的往來交流上，重要性不亞於研究成果的報告發表。本書介紹各類英文技術信函的特徵及寫作指引，所附範例中肯實用，爲優良的學習及參考書籍。

廖俊臣—國立清華大學理學院院長

本書提供許多有關工業技術合作、技術轉移 、工業資訊 、人員訓練及互訪等接洽信函的例句和範例，頗爲實用，極具參考價值。

于樹偉—工業安全衛生技術發展中心主任

國際間往來日益頻繁，以英文有效地溝通交流，是現今從事科技研究人員所 需具備的重要技能。本書在寫作風格、文法結構與取材等方面，提供極佳的寫作參考與指引，所列舉的範例，皆經過作者細心的修訂與潤飾，必能切合讀者的實際需要。

特　　價　新台幣 250 元
劃　　撥　19419482　清蔚科技股份有限公司
線上訂購　四方書網　www.4book.com.tw
發 行 所　華香園出版社　印行

The Chinese On-line Writing Lab OWL

柯泰德線上英文論文編修訓練服務

http://mx.nthu.edu.tw/~tedknoy

您有科技英文寫作上的困擾嗎？

您的文章在投稿時常被國外論文審核人員批評文法很爛嗎？以至於被退稿嗎？

您對論文段落的時式使用上常混淆不清嗎？

您在寫作論文時同一個動詞或名詞常常重複使用嗎？

您的這些煩惱現在均可透過*柯泰德網路線上科技英文論文編修服務*來替您加以解決。本服務項目分別含括如下：

　　1.英文論文編輯與修改

　　2.科技英文寫作開課訓練服務

　　3.線上寫作家教

　　4.免費寫作格式建議服務，及網頁問題討論區解答

另外，為能廣為服務中國人士對論文寫作上之缺點，柯泰德先生亦同時著作下列參考書籍可供有志人士作為寫作上之參考。

　　〈1.精通科技論文(報告)寫作之捷徑

　　〈2.做好英文會議簡報

　　〈3.英文信函參考手冊

上部份亦可由柯泰德先生的首頁中下載得到。

如果您對本服務有興趣的話，可參考柯泰德先生的首頁展示。

柯泰德網路線上科技英文論文編修服務

地址：新竹市大學路50號8樓之三

TEL:03-5724895

FAX:03-5724938

網址：http://mx.nthu.edu.tw/~tedknoy

E-mail:tedknoy@ms11.hinet.net

備註：您若有英文論文需要柯先生修改，請直接將文件以電子郵寄(E-mail)的方式，寄至上面地址，建議以WORD存檔；您也可以把存有您文件的小磁碟片（1.44MB規格）以一般郵政的方式寄達。不論您採用那種方式，都請註明您的大名及聯絡電話，以及所選文件修改的速度(5日內或10日內完成)。有任何問題，請隨時來電，謝謝。

國家圖書館出版品預行編目資料

科技英文編修手冊 / 柯泰德 (Ted Knoy) 作　—初版—

新竹市：清蔚科技，2000【民89】

面；21x29.7公分 (科技英文寫作系列；4)

譯自：An Editing Workbook for Chinese Technical Writers

ISBN 957-97544-1-1 (平裝附磁片)

1.英國語言 - 寫作法　2.論文寫作法

805.17　　　　　　　　　　　　89000351

科技英文寫作系列四

科技英文編修訓練手冊

作　　者／ 柯泰德 (Ted Knoy)

發 行 人／ 徐明哲

法律顧問／ 志揚國際法律事務所

發 行 所／ 清蔚科技股份有限公司

網　　址／ http://www.supermbox.com.tw/4book

電子郵件／ 4book@Cweb.com.tw

地　　址／ 台北市106大安區信義路4段98號5F

電　　話／ 02-2703-3898

傳　　真／ 02-2703-4127

印 刷 所／ 馨視覺編印中心

美工設計／ 陳偉婷

打字排版／ 陳偉婷

版　　次／ 2000年2月初版　2005年12月2刷

國際書碼／ ISBN 957-97544-1-1 (本書附磁片)

建議售價／ 250元

劃撥帳號／ 帳戶　清蔚科技股份有限公司

　　　　　　帳號　19419482

四方書網 http://www.4book.com.tw